THE

RAMSES

SCARAB

BY RICHARD NORMAN

A DAN GOOD MYSTERY

*Dedicated to my beloved wife Jo
who always made me feel like I was
the luckiest man in the world.*

FORWORD

It was a very different world in 1985. Modern electronic devices were in their early infancy, no cell phones or laptops, and computers were monstrous, phones were attached to the wall, phone booths were everywhere.

I wrote this book in my 90th year.

This is a work of pure fiction. No names are intentionally used of anyone living or dead.

CONTENTS

PROLOGUE
Egypt, 1213 B.C.

"You're filthy and exhausted," said Betrest, "why don't you stop for a while? You need to rest and drink some water." Nineteen-year-old Maherpa, clothed only in a white linin kilt, was so covered with dirt and limestone grime that the color of his dark bare chest and limbs was not discernable. His twin sister, Betrest, was dressed in a linin kalarsis, a very colorful shift-like dress with two straps, but she, too, was covered like her brother in grime. Both were barefoot.

"Not now, Betrest," he said, "I feel I'm getting very close."

Ramses II had been dead and buried for only a month, and Maherpa intended to be the first grave robber to rob the tomb. Robbing the tombs of the Pharaohs had been a problem for centuries in Egypt. So it was that priests were indeed watching it. Maherpa knew it was being watched but thought he had chosen a place to dig where it wasn't being watched. He wanted to be the first, so he could choose the best of the wealth that was buried with the Pharaoh; treasures Ramses II had chosen to take with him to the afterlife.

It took only another half-hour digging for Maherpa to break through into the tomb. Then it took only a few more minutes to make the opening large enough for him and Betrest to get inside.

When they finally scrambled in and held their torches high, the size of the great room astounded him and Betrest. Maherpa gasped. "This must be the great room. Just look at the size of it. It's huge!"

"I've heard people talk," said Betrest, "some say this is the largest tomb of all the pharaohs, others have said it's not. But just look at how elaborately it is decorated! Even the ceiling!" Betrest looked around in awe. They began walking around the room, mouths agape.

"And look at the hieroglyphics on the walls; the Book of the Dead is copied there, and there the Book of the Gates, and there is the Book of the Heavenly Cow. Gold is everywhere, Betrest! Amazing! We'll be rich!"

"Here is the Litany of Ra and Imydwat," said Betrest, "and here is the Opening of the mouth Ritual."

Many Egyptian deities and kings were depicted in huge statues that lined both sides of the room. Most were of Ramses II himself. He had erected so many great statues of himself over his long life, they were everywhere in Egypt.

The room branched out into three sloping corridors to a pillared chamber and two side chambers, but Maherpa was intent on finding the burial chamber, and took the slope in the center of the great room which opened to two long corridors that lead to another chamber where they veered right into the corridor that led them to the burial chamber.

In the burial chamber there were dozens of gold vessels and funerary pieces all around them, each of great value. Betrest had the big cloth sacks over her shoulder. Each took one and began stuffing objects of gold in them.

When they were satisfied their sacks were as about as full as they could carry out of the tomb, Maherpa said, "Help me a minute Betrest," as he set his sack on the floor. "I want to open the sarcophagus. The best things are usually buried with the mummy."

Betrest knew better than to cross her twin brother, though the very thought of seeing Ramses II's mummy was sickening to her. "Just look at the jewels, carvings and markings on the sarcophagus, Maherpa!" she exclaimed.

It took a good while and great effort to get it open, but it was well worth their while. Indeed, the best was with his mummified body; things Ramses II wanted to take with him to the afterlife.

When Maherpa found the huge scarab resting on Ramses' chest over his heart, he was surprised, but knew immediately that this scarab was worth a fortune. It was the largest he had ever seen. Scarabs were the symbolic epitome of life after death, and he knew there were thousands of them everywhere in Egypt, many were quite ordinary; some small, some large, but some were ornately decorated with precious stones. Ramses' scarab was not only the largest he had ever seen, but it was solid gold and more bejeweled than any he'd ever heard of. He knew he had to take it! But as his hand drew near, he saw a small scroll of papyri prominently displayed close to the scarab. He picked up the tiny scroll and opened it. It read: "The curse of the Ramses scarab is painful death to any who take it." The curse terrified him, nevertheless, he had to take it no matter. It was the most valuable treasure in the entire tomb. Though his hand began trembling, he snatched it and the small scroll quickly. Then Maherpa and Betrest scampered out of the tomb as fast as they could with their treasure sacks.

Ammon, priest of Ptah, the god of crafts, stood secluded behind a cluster of three palm trees not far from the tunnel entrance Maherpa had dug, and saw the young grave robbers emerge with their sacks of bounty and run into the night. He had been watching each night from the time Maherpa began digging his tunnel but decided not to stop them. It was his desire to obtain the treasures for himself and would let the twins do all the work to get them. He knew the twins, knew their family and where they lived, in a small humble mud-brick house. He would visit them before morning light.

When Maherpa and Betrest approached their humble abode, they stopped running and began walking as quietly as they could. Very softly Maherpa whispered to Betrest, "We must hide our treasures in the sand away from our dwelling, Betrest. We can get them later when we are ready to try to sell them."

Betrest nodded. The moon was bright. He found a hoe tool lying in the yard, and they went a good distance from the house where stood a palm tree. He dug a deep hole where they buried their treasure sacks. After the hole was covered to Maherpa's satisfaction, they sneaked into their home to their separate sleeping areas. Their house was quite small, so their straw mats for sleeping were in the same room but divided by a thick cloth which hung from one wall to the other.

Neither could sleep. They were far too excited from their illegal adventure, so they lay on their straw mats and stared into the darkness. Eventually they slept.

An hour later, Ammon, slipped silently into the house and surprised Maherpa. He laid his knife blade across Maherpa's throat and whispered softly, "Tell me where you hid your treasure sacks, or I will slit your throat. And be sure you do not wake Betrest or your parents."

Maherpa, suddenly awake, was wide eyed with terror. It was all he could do not to scream, but after a moment to compose himself, he whispered, "Never." Ammon slit his throat so swiftly and deeply that Maherpa never made a sound. The knife was so razor sharp it almost severed his head.

Then, Ammon slipped into Betrest's quarters where he woke her in like manner as he had surprised Maherpa. She woke immediately when he laid the blade across her throat, eyes wide with terror, but his warning to make no sound kept her silent. He whispered, "Tell me where you hid your sacks of treasure, or I will cut your throat. Your twin is dead because he refused me." Her eyes filled with tears and she began sobbing quietly. "Tell me!" He urged her with the slightest pressure on her throat. Betrest whispered, "I won't."

Now Ammon had a dilemma. If he killed her, she could not tell him, and if he didn't, she would surely report him to the authorities. To preserve his own life, he cut her throat as he had Maherpa's.

Ammon felt certain he could find where Maherpa had buried the treasures. As a high priest, he had been among the embalmers of Ramses' body. He knew about the scarab, that it was more valuable than the rest of the treasures combined. He had to find it. Ammon slipped away in the night. He was surprised how quickly he found the fresh mound of dirt by that palm tree. Thus, the curse of the Ramses scarab began.

Chapter 1

FOR WHOM THE WEDDING BELLS TOLL

Tuesday morning, April 23, 1985, Jerusalem, Israel.

Dan Good, an ex-CIA agent, working a case for the CIA as a freelancer, recently completed his assignment in Israel, and was about to return to his private investigator business in Dallas, Texas, but something had happened that required the help of friends who had become involved in the case, too, Alex and Bren Campbell. They were all under assumed names. He and his new found friend, Kathleen Fuller, were Mr. and Mrs. Strange The Campbells were in the hotel suite next door under the name Mr. and Mrs. Witherspoon, so he called them.

Alex conversed with him a few moments and hung up. He turned to his wife, Bren, frowned and said, "I just got the strangest phone call."

"Who was it?"

"Our strange neighbor, Mr. Strange."

"There's door between their suit and ours, why didn't he just knock and come in?"

"That's what I wondered. He want's that we meet him and Kathleen in the hall and go to breakfast with them."

"How odd. Wonder what's up."

"Well, if you are ready for breakfast, we can go find out."

"Let's go, I'm starved. I haven't eaten since dinner last night."

They met Dan and Kathleen in the hall, greeted one another, and headed for the elevator to go up to the restaurant on the top floor.

When Dan punched the elevator button, Alex asked, "What is all the mystery this morning, Dan?"

"It's a longish story. I'll tell you at breakfast."

"Okaaaaaay," said Alex, and everyone was silent until they were seated and had ordered breakfast.

"Now, big fellow, tell us your longish story," said Alex with a smile.

"Well," began Dan, "Kathleen and I talked all night, Alex. Just before bedtime, I told Kathleen that I'd fallen in love with her from the time we met. She also told me the same. Now since her husband has died, we can marry, so I popped the question and she said yes. And since you are a minister, we want you to perform our wedding on June 4th. Will you? Can you?"

"Of course, I can and will. I don't have to be a minister. In Texas, anyone can perform a wedding for anyone."

"I didn't know that. Great," Dan turned to look at Kathleen.

That was when Bren noticed how their eyes glowed with love for each other. "I knew it all along," she said, clapping her hands once. "I saw it coming ever since we found each other in Israel. I could see it in your eyes and in your mannerisms toward each other."

Kathleen was delighted to hear Bren's obvious approval. "We plan to live separately in our own homes and date until our wedding."

"That's a wonderful idea," said Alex.

"It was a wonderful, though exciting adventure we've had in Israel, thwarting *"The Megiddo Alliance,"* Kathleen said.

"The bombing of the Dome of the Rock could not have been stopped were it not for you two and Kathleen," said Dan.

The two couples truly enjoyed their time eating and talking, laughing and joking together. They had become close friends.

Then they went back to their suites to pack for their flights back to the US, and to

Dallas. Their flight left Ben Gurion Airport in Jerusalem at two. If they were lucky and there were no delays, they would all land in Dallas tomorrow about 6 A.M. or so.

The next morning, Kathleen left DFW airport to go back to her home in far north Plano, a Dallas suburb to the north of Dallas. She would continue to live in the home she and David Wayne Fuller had shared when they were married; before he committed suicide.

Dan lived in a mansion on Turtle Creek Blvd. in Highland Park; one of the two "Park Cities" surrounded by Dallas. The Campbells returned to their mansion just a few houses away from Dan on Turtle Creek Blvd.

Over the next five days, Dan and Kathleen dated every day, spending most of their dates just talking with each other; getting to know each other very well, and making plans for their wedding.

One evening, as the day drew near, Dan asked Kathleen where she wanted to go for her honeymoon. Of course, with Dan being so wealthy, she could choose anywhere in the world.

Kathleen surprised him when she answered, "I want to go to Egypt."

Dan was floored. "You want to go to Egypt?"

"Yes, we've been to Paris and Israel. David and I went to Hawaii, and I've been to the Bahamas and other places, but I've always wanted to go to Egypt, even as a young girl."

"Why? Why Egypt, of all places?"

"Because, I learned so much about it in Sunday school when I was a child. I was so interested in Egypt, too, in school when I learned about the pyramids and the Sphinx and all. Egypt has always fascinated me. I want to go see those things in person. Oh, Dan, is that so terrible?"

"Not at all, sweetheart, just surprising. Egypt it is, then."

Alex had arranged to use a big handsome church building on Skillman Avenue, and Bren helped Kathleen with planning the wedding.

Of course, Bren would be her bridesmaid since they had become best friends. Bren also helped Kathleen select bridesmaids, and helped her pick her wedding dress, and all the other details.

Alex also arranged for the music to be sung by an a-cappella chorus and soloists, including the wedding march and recessional. Also, the chorus and soloists would also sing for the reception. A most unusual wedding.

Dan's best friend was Walter Ellis, Director of the CIA, but he was to give the bride away. Jack Chenault flew in from Paris with his wife and twins. He would be Dan's Best Man.

On Tuesday evening June 4th, the wedding went without a hitch, as Alex tied the knot quite securely for his friends. It was a beautiful wedding.

Their wedding night was spent in The Mansion, that fancy hotel not far from Dan's house, where Dan took her the night they met in March, just three months ago. On Wednesday morning of June 5, 1985, Dan and Kathleen boarded a plane bound for Cairo, Egypt.

Chapter 2

A DONE DEAL

Austin, Texas, Tuesday evening, June 1, 1985.

Just at dusk on a high, craggy, limestone overlook of Lake Austin on Mount Bonnell, a dusty Ford Country Squire station wagon turned off the road and parked beside a parked white Lincoln Continental. A tall, thin man in a rumpled seersucker suit emerged from the station wagon carrying an attaché. He slipped into the front passenger seat of the Lincoln. The driver of the Lincoln flipped on the dome light and turned toward his visitor.

"You're late."

"What I have to show you is well worth your wait, so prepare yourself, my friend."

"Alright, alright," replied the short, overweight driver of the Lincoln, "Show me, please."

"Yes. Prepare yourself for a most extraordinary discovery. As I told you on the phone, I returned from my archeological dig in the ancient city of Luxor just yesterday. While I was there, I contacted my private scarab broker in Cairo as always, looking for other scarabs you might want in your collection. He gave me this copy of a black and white photograph." He then opened his attaché, and took out a single sheet of paper, handing it to the older man.

"It is the most extraordinary scarab ever discovered in history. This is the scarab of Ramses II."

The older man moved closer to the light to scrutinize it intently. The copy of the photograph showed the scarab next to a ballpoint pen. "I've only heard the legend of that scarab. This is incredible! I've never seen one so large."

"Nor has anyone else, my friend, but I have more to tell you. There are documents that have also been recently found that tell about this scarab and its history, though none of these things have been seen for over 3,000 years. They were all found by an amateur university student archeology student. He was working in a dig separate from his other students from his university. He kept them secret from his teacher and the other students. No one knows the scarab has been found. The student revealed his discovery only to my source, giving him only a copy of a photograph. This is a photo of that photo. The student wants to sell the scarab and the documents, and asked my broker to buy them from him. My broker agreed but asked for time to get the money. The boy wanted $10,000.00. I've been asked by my source to find a buyer, so I immediately thought of you. You are the only one I know who can get the cash.

"Please," said the older man, "tell me more about the scarab." He was agitated, and perspiration suddenly appeared above his upper lip. He began to salivate.

"The story is that an ancient artisan created a scarab for Ramses II. Ramses required his scarab to be the largest and most valuable scarab ever created. It was made and delivered to Ramses II in his 89th year of life.

"Look at the picture, my friend and try to imagine. It is solid gold, six inches long, four and a half inches wide, and three inches thick. There are hieroglyphics and artistic designs engraved on the gold body, and many precious gems embedded into the body."

"You don't actually possess this scarab?"

"I don't, but I can get it. There is more to this story if you wish to hear it."

"Yes, yes, of course I do. Go on, please," the older man said as he grew more excited and intense.

"What I tell you now is not just fascinating, but compelling. It has to do with the eccentricities of Ramses the Great in his last years. These are not merely legends, but documented history. Ramses II became quite obsessed with the afterlife, and believed that the finer the scarab, the greater his chances of crossing over to the other side, and he believed the gods would be more willing to welcome him into the afterlife if his scarab was exceptionally beautiful and great. Ramses also insisted his scarab be placed over his heart in the sarcophagus.

"All the great tombs of the Pharaohs, you know, have been plagued with grave robbers from the very beginning, so Ramses II attempted to add protection to his great scarab by attaching a curse of death to thieves. It was inscribed on a parchment which was found next to the scarab. The curse says that anyone taking possession of it will die a violent death."

"I don't believe in curses," grumbled the old man with disdain.

"Nor do I, Mr. Case, but I must tell you that legend has it that the grave robber who stole the Ramses scarab suffered a violent death."

"I just don't believe such hog-wash," Case scoffed.

"Of course. It is a mere legend," he conceded. "Nevertheless, there you have it." The professor turned in his seat to face forward into the gathering darkness.

Resignedly, Case asked, "How much is it going to cost me?"

"One million dollars including finder's fees. Cash."

"Done! Get it for me."

Chapter 3

THE HONEYMOONERS

Friday morning, June 7, 1985, Cairo, Egypt.

"The wind blew my hair, and I don't like blue hair," Dan said frowning as he came through the door of their hotel suite.

Kathleen, sitting on the couch, giggled and said, as though speaking baby-talk to a small child, "Well, come here sweetheart. I'll sew your hair back on for you." He handed her his pocket comb. "You're going to have to sit down or bend down for me, big guy." She stood as he sat on the couch.

"Looks like you combed it with a pillow, but I can fix it." And with a few strokes, she said, "There. All better now?" and she handed his comb back.

"Thanks, honey. It's a fair morning for some shopping. The wind is supposed to die down soon. Are you ready to go, it's almost nine o'clock, the bazaars should be buzzing and busy by now?"

"Right with you, let me grab my purse," and she headed for the bedroom.

Dan had booked them into a luxury suite at the Nile Ritz-Carlton with expansive views of the beautiful Nile River and the remarkable city of Cairo from the sixth floor. "Our flight to Luxor doesn't leave until four-twenty this afternoon," he called after her. He looked out the window at a tall minaret where the calls for Muslim prayers resounded five times a day.

"Great," she said emerging from the bedroom purse in hand.

Dan Good looked with pride at his new bride with her long natural blond hair falling gently just below her shoulders, and her lovely face aglow and love twinkling in her light blue eyes. "I love you. You look gorgeous!"

"I love you, too." She kissed him on the lips briefly, then headed for the door. Dan opened it for her and followed, locking it behind them.

The newlyweds walked hand in hand in the Souk market, Kahn El Khalili, in the Hussein District of Cairo.

There was such an abundance of color everywhere she looked. Kathleen was dazzled by it all in all the wonderful shops on either side of the narrow street. There were no cars, of course, but it was crowded with shoppers, and tourists milling about.

She tugged Dan over to a shop and fingered the fine, brightly colored, handmade fabrics. "These fabrics are fabulous, Dan. The quality and colors. I just must have some. You know how I love to sew and make my own clothes."

"Buy all you want, my love," he said.

She made several purchases. Kathleen was an excellent seamstress. She had made the dress she was wearing. Of course, with the new fabrics she would also need to buy some shoes, gloves, and a purse (or three), and a couple of broad-brimmed hats to go with the lovely fabric. Dan was soon burdened with her purchases. As they passed farther along the bazaar, Dan stopped at a small jewelry shop to examine something that caught his eye. Funny looking little things he'd never seen before. He had no idea what the little objects were, but several were filigreed with carved decorations, and small, fine stones, rubies, amethysts, emeralds, topaz, and diamonds.

"Look, Kathleen, what are these?"

"What?" She sidled close to him to look.

The shopkeeper suddenly appeared before them, "They are scarabs," he said. "They are amulets, sir," the old man said in broken English. "They were very sacred in

Ancient Egypt, especially in the time of the pharaohs, and still are for many today."

"They look like bugs," Kathleen said, wrinkling her nose and bending closer to the display to examine the collection in the glass display counter.

The old shopkeeper replied as he picked one up, "They are Egyptian symbols in the form of beetles. The most common scarabs are rings, though some are amulets worn around the neck on a chain like beads as mere ornaments. Some are broaches made for women. The rings often bear Egyptian hieroglyphs, and some were used as seals for letters and documents."

"Why beetles?" asked Dan.

"Scarab is derived from the Latin word scarabaeus, meaning literally, beetle. The female dung beetle rolls bits of dung until it gets round and firm, then lays her eggs in it. The baby beetle, when it is born, then eats the dung until it is grown, and the dung is gone."

"Dung! Yuck!" Kathleen exclaimed with a grimace, but the old man, ignoring her, continued.

"It symbolizes Ra, the god Khenri, the Egyptian sun god, who renews the sun each morning, rolls it across the sky and back down into the horizon. Then he carries it through the other world, and renews the sun the next morning, thus scarabs symbolize eternity. They protect the living and carry them after death into the afterlife."

"Look at this bigger one, Dan, it has some inscription on it, and it is decorated with precious stones." Looking up at the older man, she asked, "What is its value?"

The old man frowned and said, "That one is priced at $1,000.00. Most are quite inexpensive. Some do not have precious stones, but fakes. Such are mere baubles. There are many fake scarabs, I'm sorry to say. He pointed to one, "That one is only $2.00 American, but I have many authentic scarabs that begin as low as $10.00 American, but they are small and without jewels." Then, he looked Kathleen and brightened. "I do have something very special that I bought last night. You might like it if you will wait till I bring it out." And with amazing agility for his age, he swiftly went through a divided curtain at the back of his little shop, returning in very few minutes. In his right hand he carried a soft cloth.

"This one is a precious scarab. It is larger than most, and expensive," he said as he opened the cloth to reveal the dazzling jeweled scarab. It was about two inches long.

"It's beautiful!" Kathleen said. "Stunning!" It must cost a small fortune."

Dan had been observing the exchange between them, and spoke, "What is its price, if I may ask?."

The old shopkeeper and Kathleen suddenly turned to look at Dan as though they had forgotten he was present.

"Perhaps $1,500.00 American, more or less. I am willing to negotiate a price if you like. I just wanted the young lady to see it," he said speaking softly and with a deeply furrowed brow.

Grinning, Dan said to the old shopkeeper, "I'll give you $500.00 dollars, American."

The old man squinted at him, "$1,000.00," he countered. "But no less." Dan countered, "$900.00, but not a penny more."

Kathleen grabbed Dan's arm saying, "Dan! You can't mean it, sweetheart."

He winked at her, "No, I'm not about to buy it. Thank you, sir, but I've no interest in scarabs. Let's go, honey." They went next door to a rug shop.

The old man frowned and mumbled to himself, "As I expected, but I always hope." He wrapped the scarab in the soft cloth and turned to return it to its hiding place. "Cursed Americans."

As they walked slowly, Kathleen leaned closer to Dan and said softly, "That was not much of a jewelry store, it was mostly just costume jewelry, baubles, but lots of scarabs." Then, she wrapped both her arms around Dan's arm, drawing herself closer to him, whispering, "That old man looked like he'd had bad news as a child and has never gotten over it." She grinned up at him.

"S'nuff," Dan said, "S'nuff of that nonsense," he chuckled. "You're vicious, you know that? That poor old man."

She laughed and then turned serious. "You know something? I'm so happy to be married to a man that I can just be my silly self with. I love you so much, Dan."

He looked down into her eyes and said, tenderly, "I never dreamed I would find a girl I couldn't live without, but I did when I found you. And I think we've shopped enough. I don't think I can carry much more, let's go back to our hotel," he suggested with a wry smile, and a twinkle in his eyes. He quickened his pace with long strides, almost dragging her.

She knew exactly what he had in mind. Kathleen, at five-foot-eleven, scurried to keep pace with her six-nine husband. "The trouble is," she said, "you don't get shorter wearing flats like I do."

Nekhtou closed his little jewelry shop in the bazaar earlier than usual, and scurried to his car, a very fine Mercedes Benz, and drove to the Café Riche at 17 Talaat Harb Street in downtown Cairo. His little shop in the bazaar was only a front for his very lucrative secret brokerage of Egyptian treasures.

He was fortunate to find a parking spot less than a block from the Café and entered the red doors where he quickly spotted the professor in his wrinkled seersucker suit seated near the kitchen area. The professor stood to greet his visitor, and they sat.

"I have just been seated, so haven't ordered yet, but the waiter gave me two minus," he said as he handed one to Nekhtou.

"Thank you, but I just want a cup of karkaday."

"Their roast beef is very good; it comes with pasta."

"Perhaps later, it is much too early for supper for me."

Just then, their waiter appeared. The professor ordered the roast beef and a beer; Nekhtou ordered his strong tea, and the waiter disappeared.

The professor said softly, "I have found a buyer."

"So soon?"

"Yes, he is a wealthy Texas lawyer, and he has agreed to your price."

Nekhtou could scarcely contain his excitement. His little side business as a broker had made him a very nice living indeed, but this... even deducting the finder's fees, I'll be richer than I ever dreamed, he thought.

"He agreed to the price?"

"Jumped on it, in fact. How soon can you take possession," asked the professor?

"I'll have the scarab tomorrow. How soon will you have the money?"

"I will have to work that out with my buyer. He is here in Cairo now. Let's meet tomorrow evening. I'll see what I can do."

"Good," said Nekhtou masking his great joy. "I'll reserve a table for us at the Koshari al-Tahrir restaurant tomorrow evening at nine."

Chapter 4

TOURING THE TOMBS

Saturday morning, June 8, 1985, Luxor, Egypt.

"Here in the Valley of the Kings are the massive and magnificent structures of ancient Egypt, the enormous monuments of the ancient Pharaohs, the great pyramids, and the tombs that were embedded deep into the limestone hills." The tour guide droned on to his crowd of tourists. He was a large, heavyset man dressed in a white suit made a little beige by the blowing sand. His black tie was askew, and his suit and white fedora were wilted by sweat.

"The New Kingdom of Egypt was ruled by the pharaohs from 1539 to 1075 B.C. The Kings are buried, of course, here in the Valley of the Kings. Their Queens are buried, as you might expect, in the Valley of the Queens. These are the burial grounds of the 18th, 19th, and 20th dynasties of Egypt's history.

"The most famous tombs are Tutankhamun, Seti I, and Ramses II, but many others are also buried here, even high priests and various elites of that era."

Dan leaned down to Kathleen's ear and said softly, "I haven't thought about that scarab until now. Wonder if the old guy's unloaded it yet."

Kathleen looked up at him. "For $1,500.00 dollars? I doubt it. Why? Do you want to buy it now?"

"I believe he'd take the $900,00 I mentioned, remember? I can't imagine paying a $1,000.00 for it, can you?"

"I can't see paying even the $500.00 you first offered him," she replied.

"I might try giving him my first offer of $500.00, but I certainly wouldn't pay more than $900.00, no matter the gems on it. Who would want such a thing, anyway?"

"You, maybe, but 'Not me, said chicken little,'" she said with a straight face. "Too much money for a bug."

The guide continued: "Into these enormous tombs carved into the ground are the most elaborate preparations for the pharaohs for the world of the afterlife where the pharaohs, who were considered gods themselves, were to become one with the gods they worshipped.

"They were mummified to keep their bodies preserved until their souls revived in the afterlife.

"You will be amazed when see the well-stocked earthly provisions deemed essential in the world beyond... unbelievable treasures and wealth... dazzling gold objects, masks, and even mundane utensils... furniture, wearing apparel, including undergarments and incredible collections of jewelry. Most of the valuable treasures are in the museum. Of course, tomb robbers have also taken many of treasures over the centuries."

Listening to the guide, Dan said, "I'm impressed."

"Me, too! Oh, Dan, What a wonderful honeymoon! *You're* wonderful!" Kathleen tugged his arm, pulling him down to kiss him on his cheek.

"Music to my ears," he replied with a smile. "I love you, Kathleen, and I plan to tell you that every day for the rest of our lives."

"A lifetime of love, darling."

"Think we're getting too mushy?"

"Not a bit of it, you doofus. Not even close."

As the crowd of tourists were about to enter the tomb of Ramses II, the tour guide said, "Ramses II's son and successor to the throne, Ramses III, is buried over there," he pointed to a tomb just opposite, across the way. "But," he continued, "this tomb,

carved into the limestone hill at Theban is
one of the largest of the Pharaohs'. It has
three sloping corridors from the great main
entry room, and you will soon see the
pillared chamber, two smaller side
chambers, and then the passage leading to
the burial chamber itself."

As they approached the entrance,
Kathleen leaned closer to Dan to speak
softly, "Just look at that entryway, Dan, it's
awesome with those great statues that seem
to be standing guard."

"Mmm," Dan said in agreement.

Inside, the guide pointed out, among
the elaborate decorations, the writings on
the wall of the great room, "The
hieroglyphics on the walls of this great room
are religious words, this one from The Book
of the Gates there, and that one is of The
Book of the Heavenly Cow, and there," he
pointed, "is the Imydwat, relating to the
religion of ancient Egypt, then here is The
Litany of Ra, the sun god, then there is The
Opening of the Mouth ritual. The great
statues along the walls are of deities and
kings, but most are statues of Ramses II
himself."

When the tour finally came to the
room which was the actual tomb, the guide
said, "Floods are what have caused most of
the damage you see in this chamber, but
grave robbers did much damage as well.
The sarcophagus itself is missing, of course.
Ramses II's mummy now resides in the Hall

of Mummy's in the Cairo Museum with other mummy's."

Dan bent down to whisper in Kathleen' ear, "I'd like to take a peek at him when we go back to Cairo tomorrow."

"No way! A mummy? Not on your life, yuk," said Kathleen. Instead, let's also go back and look at that scarab again," replied Kathleen.

"Okay, I might buy it for you as a memento of our honeymoon."

"I would love that sweetheart!" Kathleen was thrilled.

They returned to their hotel room in Luxor and ordered room service for when it came time for dinner. Now, relaxing outside on their balcony, in very comfortable reclining chairs, side by side, they held hands as the bright moonlight of an almost full moon seemed to fill the sky. They sat for a long time in comfortable silence, enjoying just being together in beautiful surroundings.

Kathleen eventually broke the silence. "I had a great time today, in spite of the heat and sand. And it is so nice that neither of us feels like we have to entertain the other. It is relaxing."

"I know, I was just thinking the same thing. Of course, we Texans are used to the heat."

"Right," said Kathleen, "but the sand was awful! Next time I'll wear boots instead of barefoot sandals."

Then, Kathleen added, changing the subject, "I was exhausted after our tour, but I'm better now, wanna 'squiggle?'"

Chapter 5

JUSTIN CASE

Sunday morning, June 9, 1985, Luxor, Egypt.

"Oh, no!"

"What?" said Kathleen.

Dan grimaced, "Our plane back to Cairo is an old 'puddle-jumper,' an old DC-3 from the days of WWII. I can barely get in one, no room for my legs."

"Maybe your legs can catch the next flight."

"Funny," said Dan. "The flight is less than an hour, I'll endure it."

The plane they'd come to Luxor in was a very nice small jet, no first-class seating, but comfortable enough for Dan. The DC-3 was crowded, so Dan and Kathleen nudged their way down the sloping aisle to their assigned seats. There was no first-class seating with larger seats for the needs of Dan's long legs.

Kathleen slipped into her window seat with Dan squeezing into the aisle seat beside her, so he could later poke his size 14s into the aisle. There were two seats along their side of the cabin, and single seats along the other side.

Dan noticed every seat taken except the one directly across the aisle from him. In a few minutes, things began to settle down, but there was still a lot of jabbering in a variety of languages. Dan turned toward Kathleen who was settled comfortably, and said, "Hear that? They're jabbering in gibberish?"

She grinned and asked, "Is they speaking in Patagonian, or Mongohelian?"

"A little of both, I'm sure."

Kathleen's eyes drifted to notice a man scurrying down the aisle. He was in his late 60s at least, she figured, perhaps only 5'5" or there about, and quite overweight. He sat in the seat across the aisle from Dan, and Kathleen stretched to speak into Dan's ear to whisper, "Did you see the man who just sat across from you?"

"I did. I assume you noticed the same thing I did?"

"He's wearing a scarab amulet around his neck."

"Right. Nothing very fancy, but a pretty nice one that I expect he paid a good price for. I'm going to ask him about it, but

I'm going to wait until we're airborne before I do."

When the plane leveled off in its flying altitude, Dan leaned across the aisle, touching the man's arm to get his attention. He virtually had to shout to be heard above the propeller driven twin engines. "I beg your pardon, sir, but I noticed the amulet you're wearing, it's a scarab isn't it?"

"Yes, it is," the man replied, smiling, but said nothing more.

"I'm curious about it. I saw some scarabs in a bazar in Cairo, is that where you bought it?"

The older man picked it up to look at it, holding it so Dan could see it, too. "I bought this one from a private dealer in Cairo that I know. I do most of my business with him. Are you a collector, too?"

"A collector?" Dan asked with surprise. "No, I'm not a collector, but I would like to visit with you when we land in Cairo, would you join us for lunch? Our treat? Perhaps in the restaurant of our hotel, the Nile Ritz-Carlton?"

"Thank you, that would be fine, that's where I'm staying. I would enjoy that very much."

"It's a bit hard to converse in these circumstances," Dan said.

The older man nodded, "Yes. Prop-planes are so loud. Can I meet you folks in the restaurant after we settle into the hotel?"

"That would be great. My name is Good, Dan Good, my wife's Kathleen, by the way."

"Glad to meet you, my name is Case."

"What about meeting about one p.m. for lunch, Mr. Case, is that too late?"

"No, that would be fine, Mr. Good."

"Just call us Dan and Kathleen, please."

Case just smiled and nodded.

Their conversation ended, and Dan turned to Kathleen, "We are to lunch with our new friend when we land, a Mr. Case."

Kathleen grinned and said, "Great. Looking forward to meeting him. I want to know about his scarab."

"He is a collector of scarabs."

"You're kidding, right?"

"No, not at all."

"A collector? This will be interesting," said Kathleen.

The NOX Restaurant, named after the Goddess of the Night, is located on the top floor of the NILE Ritz-Carlton Hotel. When they arrived at the entryway, Dan, being so tall, easily spotted Mr. Case seated at a table nearby. He waved away the Maitre'D as he guided Kathleen to where Mr. Case was seated, menu in hand and two more on his table.

"Mr. Case, I'd like you to meet my wife, Kathleen, we're newlyweds, three days now," he said with pride.

Case stood and politely shook her hand. "So happy to meet you, Mrs. Good. I was early, so I got us a table."

"Perfect," Dan said as he helped his bride into her seat.

Case stood until Kathleen was seated. When he sat back down, Kathleen reached to lay her hand on Mr. Case's arm for a moment as she said, "I'm so happy to finally meet you, Dan and I live in Dallas, where are you from; I can tell you are Texan from your accent."

"I've lived in Austin all my life, born and raised there."

"And, may I ask what you do in Austin," said Dan picking up his menu?

"I've retired just last month. I have a law firm there; my daughter is also a lawyer and now has taken over since my retirement."

"How nice," said Kathleen, "What is your field of law, sir?"

"Criminal law," he answered. "And what do you do, Mr. Good?"

"I have a private detective agency in Dallas, THE GOOD INVESTIGATORS. It is the largest in Dallas."

"I see," said Case, "And what do you detect?"

"Mostly the usual things private eyes do, infidelities, missing persons, and the like."

All three of them were finished studying their menus and set them down. Their waiter suddenly appeared and said in heavily accented English, "Would you like to order drinks, and an appetizer?"

Case ordered their house wine, Dan said, "My wife and I would like iced tea, please. No appetizer for us, thank you "

"Nor for me," said Case. The waiter raised his eyebrows slightly, "Of course. I shall be back soon with your drinks," and he disappeared.

Kathleen handed Dan her menu. "Just order me some kind of salad, please, sweetheart."

When the waiter returned with their drinks, he took their orders and left. Then Dan said, "About your scarab, Mr. Case... "

Case interrupted, "I think we can all be on a first name basis now, just call me Justin."

It was all Dan and Kathleen could do to keep from laughing. Dan said as soberly as he could, "Your name is Justin Case?"

"I know. It's ridiculous, but true. Incredible isn't it to be stuck with a name like that. I've been laughed at all my life, but the interesting thing is that I have put it to my advantage as a lawyer."

Kathleen smiled, "Oh, really?"

"Yes," Case answered, taking a couple of business cards from his jacket pocket and handing them each one.

His card read, "JUSTIN CASE," and under his name, the line: "YOU NEED A LAWYER."

"That is so clever of you, Justin," said Kathleen.

"Not my cleverness, I'm sorry to say, but that of my advertising agency. As I said, I retired, so my daughter has taken the helm now. However, the cleverness continues with her. You see, her name is Ann Justin Case." He smiled broadly.

Dan turned the conversation back to the scarabs, "How did you become a collector of scarabs, Justin?"

"Well before I retired, I began having health issues, so I went to my doctor. He said my problem was stress. Being a criminal lawyer can be quite stressful."

"I can just imagine," responded Dan.

"Yes. My doctor said I should take some time off, go for a long vacation, or, he suggested, I could take up a hobby. I didn't want to take off work, I was very busy, so I asked him, 'What kind of hobby?' He said, 'I don't know, collecting stamps, fishing, or you could do what I do, collect scarabs.' Well, I'd never heard of scarabs, so I asked about them. So he told me, and he showed me some of his collection he had in his office. I was very intrigued. He then offered to help me become a collector. He put me in touch with his broker, a professor of archeology at Texas University in Austin. Over the past several months, I have spent quite a bit of money, and now have a very respectable collection. That was why I came to Egypt. You've seen my latest scarab."

"That is very interesting, Justin," said Dan.

Case nodded, "You might be interested to know of a scarab I just learned of recently. It was just discovered in an excavation in an ancient garbage dump near the city of Luxor in Egypt. It is called, the Ramses Scarab.

"We just visited the Valley of the Kings," interjected Kathleen.

Case merely smiled at her and continued, "It is far and away the largest and most valuable scarab in the world. It's solid gold, very ornate and bejeweled, plus there is the ancient story that surrounds it. The story is what has helped make it so valuable."

"Tell us, please," said Kathleen.

"Well. According to my broker, Ramses II, in his later life, became obsessed with the concept of the afterlife as believed by the ancient Egyptians, but his concept exceeded the norm. Ramses the Great, as he became known, believed that his scarab would guarantee him eternal life if he made it so elaborate as to impress his Egyptian gods that they would welcome him into the afterlife. So, he had Egypt's finest artisans to create the largest and most elaborately designed and decorated scarab ever made, and he demanded it be placed over his heart in death to transport him to the afterlife."

"What an amazing story," said Dan. I had no knowledge of such ancient beliefs."

"There is a curse of death attached to the Ramses scarab, and legend claims that all who have possessed it met a horrible and violent death. But all that is mere fabrication, I expect. There is no such history of such a curse."

Justin Case continued to regale his newfound friends with several other stories and beliefs involving scarabs. More, actually, than they really wanted to know. Then, Case told them that he intended to buy the Ramses scarab. He would soon make an appointment with his private dealer to make the purchase while he was here in Egypt.

After their lunch, Dan and Kathleen went back to their suite. When Dan had closed the door, Kathleen said, "He's a well-heeled lawyer, that Justin Case, to be able to squander big bucks on a bug."

"True," said Dan, "I wouldn't on just a hobby."

"Honey," said Kathleen, "I am anxious to see that scarab again."

"Anything you wish my princess."

"I do have one other wish," she tilted her head and grinned.

It was midafternoon when Dan and Kathleen returned to the shop to find the old man just wrapping up a sale, so they waited. When he was finished, Dan said, "Sir. We'd like to see that scarab again if we may. I've decided to buy it."

The old man's eyes lighted up, and his face slit into a wide smile, "Certainly, sir." He quickly disappeared behind the back curtain and returned with the scarab wrapped in its soft cloth.

"Didn't you last say you would take $900.00 American for it?"

"Yes, sir. You are practically stealing it from me at that price."

"Alright, we'll take it. Do you take American Express?"

"Oh, yes, sir."

The old man carefully laid the scarab in a bag, and Kathleen said, "Thank you very much, sir." Then turning to Dan said, "Oh, Dan! Thank you, sweetheart."

"Just don't bug me about it."

She giggled.

Chapter 6

NOTHING TO WEAR

Monday morning, June 10, 1985, Cairo, Egypt.

At eight-forty-five a.m., Nekhtou Gamal entered his little shop, but did not open for business. Instead, he picked up his phone and dialed. The phone rang only once and a gruff young voice answered in English, "Hello!"

Nekhtou said in broken English, "I am ready to make the transaction. When can we meet?"

"I will come to your shop immediately," the young man replied. Nekhtou kept his shop closed and waited anxiously for his guest, a young amateur archaeologist student who arrived in less than half an hour.

"That was fast," said Nekhtou.

"I am anxious to be rid of the accursed thing. You know about the curse?"

"Of course, but that old curse doesn't scare me. It's just superstitious nonsense."

"I am not so sure. Do you have the money?"

"As agreed. There is ten thousand dollars American in this envelope. Give me the scarab, and I will give you the money."

The exchange was made, and as the young student's hand touched the envelope, he felt the long knife enter his abdomen and thrust deep and upward toward his heart. It was the last thing the young student ever knew.

Nekhtou took his blade, wiped it clean, and said, "We must keep the curse going, my young friend." He retrieved the envelope which contained only slips of paper.

Today, Nekhtou was dressed in a kaftan and keffiyeh. Of course his kaftan was bloody, and so was the area around the dead young American. So Nekhtou swiftly removed his bloody clothing and his victim's. He wrapped the naked young man tightly in the old tarpaulin that he'd been standing on, placed their bloody clothes in a bag, and put on a fresh kaftan. Now his shop showed no sign of the killing at all.

It was somewhat of a struggle for the old man to wrestle the dead man into a large yellow wicker basket, but he did. Then he was able to walk the basket out to his car. He asked Saphet, from the rug shop next to his, to help him load the basket into the trunk of his Mercedes. The trunk lid would not close completely, so he left it open and drove away.

It was a rather long drive, but Nekhtou soon found an expanse of barren desert, far from civilization. He wrestled the basket out of the car and onto the ground. The top came off the basket, and it turned over spilling the dead man partially out of it. Nekhtou rolled the body away from the basket, then with the bloody clothing in the basket, he got a gasoline can from the car trunk, poured the propane over everything, lit a match and set it all on fire. Then, he hurriedly got into his car and fled. The exposed dead body would be eaten by animals soon.

Jerry Weaver and Gina Hobby met for lunch. Jerry arrived first, secured a table where he could watch for Gina to arrive. The restaurant was far away from their hotel. Far enough that they would not be seen by their companions. They were archeology students from Princeton

University here on a dig. She had claimed to be having her period, thus not able to go with the group this morning. He claimed to have eaten something that gave him diarrhea. They had become drawn to each other on the trip to Egypt, but were trying to keep their mutual attraction secret, for Mrs. Fosbury, their professor, made it clear there must be no fraternization on this trip.

He saw her get out of her taxi, and bounce happily toward the entrance. Jerry met her at the door, noticing the brightness of her eyes, and her smile. She was beautiful in his eyes. They embraced and kissed. They'd had very few chances for such intimacy thus far.

He escorted her to their table, saying, "I'm so glad you could get away. You look gorgeous Gina."

"Thanks, cutie," she said.

Once he'd seated her, he sat across from her, and handed her one of the menus the waiter had left.

Gena said, "What do you have in mind for us today?"

"I have just the thing for our Egyptian adventure."

"Yeah?"

"Yeah. What do you think of riding a Dune Buggy in the sand dunes for a couple of hours?"

"Wow! What a novel idea, Jerry, I

think it would be fun. Just you and me?"

"Sorry, it would be too dangerous, I checked it out. We are scheduled for a group event at two this afternoon. We should be back in plenty of time not to be missed."

"Oh," she said, expressing her disappointment.

"It will be fun, I guarantee."

"Okay, I guess. We never seem to have any time for just us to get better acquainted."

"It will happen, I promise, Gina. Maybe not until we get back into our dorms."

"Sure. It is just hard to wait."

"Don't I know."

After lunch, they went for a stroll through the Souk market.

"Look, Gina, that shop has just what we need." He selected a white, wide brimmed hat for her and a man's version for himself.

"I love my hat, Jerry, thanks."

"You'll need sunglasses, too."

"No I have a pair in my clutch."

"Good. I need a pair." He selected a pair, and paid for everything.

"You paid for our lunch; I can pay for my hat."

"No, no. This whole thing was my idea, and it's our first date. It's all my treat."

"Who are you, Daddy Warbucks?"

"Don't I look like him?"

"Silly," she laughed. "You aren't bald."

She took a look in a mirror to set her hat at just right angle.

"Tell me about our adventure."

"I already made reservations for us. We need to be at Dune Buggy Tours by one to do paperwork. Then our caravan leaves at two. There will be two guides. We frolic until five and should be back by five-thirty. That should give us plenty of time to prepare before our crew returns from the dig. Tea will be available in their Bedouin tent. Our ride there and back is air conditioned. It should be lots of fun."

When they checked in at the small dune buggy establishment, they learned their group would be only seven adults, two were over sixty. The trip out took just under half an hour, and soon, Jerry and Gina were headed out together to zip around on the dunes. He let Gina be first to drive. She quickly whisked them out of sight of their group, and as she took them over a high dune, at the top she turned too sharply, and the buggy turned over, rolling down the incline. Laughing, they climbed out of the contraption to right it, and that's when Jerry saw the dead body.

"Gina," he cried. "Look, someone has been killed."

They looked at the bloody naked body of a young man not ten feet away. Scavenger birds were feasting. Gina and Jerry turned away and retched.

Jerry recovered first and said, "Come on, Gina, help me right this thing right so we can go tell our guides."

It was almost an hour before Cairo police showed up. Another hour passed before the group was allowed to return to the buggy shop. This was an adventure they would never forget.

It was half-past-three when Dan and Kathleen left the hotel for the Souk market to find the old man's small jewelry shop. As they approached, Kathleen exclaimed, "Look, Dan, his shop is closed!"

"Not exactly, honey, it looks like the police are searching it." There were several Cairo police officers milling about.

"Wonder what's going on, what's happened?"

"I'll ask, though I doubt they will tell us anything."

Dan strode up to a policeman that was standing near the shop who seemed to be in charge. "I beg your pardon, sir, but can you tell me what is going on? Why is his shop shut down, and where is the old man who owns it?"

The policeman, turned to Dan who towered above him, and answered, "We are investigating a possible robbery, you will have to shop elsewhere."

Dan persisted, "But the old man, the shopkeeper, where is he?"

"I'm sorry, but I can tell you nothing more. It is Egyptian police business. You must leave this area. We have our job to do." And he turned away as he was approached by one of his men.

Dan led Kathleen some distance away. "I don't like this. I would like to find out what's happened. I'm afraid the old man might have been killed in a robbery."

"Oh, Dan. That poor old man."

"If he is dead," he added.

"You don't believe in the curse Justin spoke of, and do you think he might have been the dealer Justin was to meet?"

"I have no idea, but I'd like to do a little investigating."

Kathleen looked at her husband of three days and said, "On our honeymoon? You have no authority to do any snooping in Egypt."

"I know, and I'm sorry, Kathleen. Just a day or two. I'll be discrete, I promise. Let me take you back to the hotel."

"Forget that. I stayed with you from

Dallas to Paris and to Israel, remember? I'm going with you wherever you go, sweetie."

"But I was trying to protect you." he protested.

"I'm not going to sit alone in a hotel on my honeymoon," she said, narrowing her eyes. "I am going with you, you big, loveable ox."

Dan was not about to argue. "Okay. Let's get back to the hotel and change into some work-clothes. I have an idea."

"I haven't a thing to wear!"

"Well, I won't let you go naked, that would cause a riot," said Dan.

Kathleen giggled, "I mean I don't know what to wear, a dress, shorts, slacks, or jeans?"

"We just want to appear as normal tourists, but why don't you wear a dress, something cool and airy for this hot Egyptian afternoon?"

"Fine."

"Keep in mind that it will not only be very hot, but sandy as well. We are in Egypt, you know."

"Think I'll wear a pale blue sundress; it will be cooler."

"Good choice, but don't wear sandals, how about loafers."

"Nope, I have some short boots.

Didn't you say something about a plan? What do you do first as an investigator in a foreign land without authority, Sherlock?"

"I don't have any idea what to expect here in Egypt, and the only crime scene I know of is the old man's shop. All I was told was that it was robbed. Don't know if I can get access to it, but I'd like to look around.

Chapter 7

A TISKET, A TASKET, A GREAT BIG
YELLOW BASKET

They took a taxi to the bazaar, then strolled through the maze of shops like the tourists they were. At the old man's shop, they found no police, nor was it cordoned off, but it was closed down.

"Looks like I'm not going to get inside without breaking and entering. Let's just stand here a few minutes. I still want to look around outside his shop."

They casually meandered around outside the shop, observing what they could, which was nothing. The Bazaar was crowded with tourists, thanks to Hosni Mubarak opening and expanding Egypt's showcase of treasures for the world to see and admire.

"I don't see anything," said Dan. "The Cairo police did a pretty good job of cleaning up. I just wish I could get inside."

Unknown to Dan and Kathleen, a small boy had been loitering nearby, observing them with keen interest. It seems that every city from time immemorial has had its share of street urchins, and this boy blended well into that group in Cairo. Therefore, Dan had taken no notice of him, but now it appeared to this boy that this couple, who seemed so interested in Nekhtou's shop, were about to leave, so he slipped up to Dan's towering stature and shook his slacks.

"Hey, mister," he said, looking up at him with his sandy face. "You wanna look inside?"

Dan looked down at a little urchin about three feet tall, and smiled. "I do indeed, young man. You have any ideas?"

"I have a key. I'm Nekhtou's nephew. He pay me to keep watch on his shop. I see what goes on."

Kathleen squatted down to his eye level. "And what's your name, if I may ask?"

He beamed her a big smile, stuck out his chest and said, "Me Aksu."

"And, what did you call him? Nek...?"

"No, Nekhtou."

That's what I thought you said," said Kathleen, laughing.

Dan bent down, "And why would you let us in, perfect strangers?"

"I think you wanna find my uncle."

Kathleen asked, "Where do you think he is?"

"I was playing down the street from the shop this afternoon, and saw him put a big basket in his trunk and drive away. He hasn't come back."

Dan said, "He could still come back, the day isn't over. How old are you, Aksu?"

"Six. My birthday was yesterday."

"Well, happy birthday, Aksu," said Kathleen.

"Where do you live, Aksu?"

The boy looked at Dan, and said, "I live with uncle Nekhtou."

"Where are your parents?"

The boy acted like he didn't hear the question. "My mother and I live with my uncle."

"How is it you have a key to his shop, young man?"

"He gave it me in case of emergencies."

"You have quite a vocabulary for a six-year-old," said Kathleen.

"Uncle Nekhtou teach me. He good teacher. I like learn English."

"Well, Aksu," Dan said as he stood up, "I would very much like to look around in the shop if you will help us. I promise we won't steal anything."

Aksu smiled and went to the entrance. He inserted the key, opened the door, and stood waiting for Dan and Kathleen to enter. He said, "I have a whistle if you try." He showed them his whistle on a chain around his neck.

"You are well prepared, my little friend," said Dan.

Inside, with all the shutters closed, the shop was dark, but Aksu quickly flipped on an overhead light.

"Thank you, young sir," Dan smiled at the child.

The inside of the shop had been tossed. By the police no doubt, thought Dan. He and Kathleen began looking through the mess.

"Oh, look, Dan, the scarabs are gone. Those thieving police!"

"Oh, no," said Aksu, "my uncle puts them in his big safe when he leaves. Never leaves them out when he goes somewhere."

"I don't suppose you have a key or know the combination."

"No, mister."

"Dan. You can call me Dan, and this is my wife, Kathleen." Dan found the large safe covered by a big piece of cloth. He examined the door. It had a combination lock.

"Well, we can't look in the safes." There was a small safe next to the big one. "Do you know what he keeps in the small safe?"

The boy frowned, "No. I know he keeps petty-cash in the little one, but there's lots of other stuff he keeps in those safes."

"Hey, Aksu, you seem too young for Nekhtou to be your uncle," said Kathleen.

The boy looked puzzled for a moment, then said, brightly, "My mother calls him uncle, too."

"Ah," said Kathleen, "he's your great uncle."

"I see several baskets around everywhere, large and small," said Dan. "How large was the basket your great uncle took, Aksu?"

The boy pointed, "The biggest, like that one."

"Wow! That is really big. What do you think was in it?"

"It very heavy," said the boy, "he had to ask his friend next door to help him get it in the trunk of his car. The car went way down in the back after it was inside."

"Hm," said Dan, thinking. "Do you know the time he drove away?"

"I don't know time yet," Aksu answered, "but I remember there were little smears of red paint around on the outside, like something spilled."

"Good observation, Aksu. Do you know the man who helped him?"

"Sure, it was Saphet. He has the shop next door. Want me to get him for you?"

"Yes, if he is still here."

Aksu took off running. Then in a very few minutes, he returned with a large, strong-looking young Egyptian man in tow. Dan and Kathleen turned to greet him. "I'm Good. Dan Good, and this is my wife, Kathleen. Thank you for coming so quickly, Saphet."

"Aksu is my little friend. I pay him to watch my shop sometimes. Happy to make your acquaintance Mr. and Mrs. Good. How can I help you?"

"Aksu said you helped Nekhtou get his basket in the trunk of his car."

"Yes, it was much too heavy for him."

"What can you tell me about the basket? Do you know what was in it?"

"No, he didn't tell me, but I can tell you it smelled badly."

"What did it smell like?"

"Like someone needed a bath very much."

"You mean, body odor?"

He nodded. "The basket was really heavy, and I wondered if someone was hiding inside."

"You thought someone was in the basket? What made you think it might be a person?"

"It was the way the weight was uneven and shifted as the basket turned. I can't think of anything else that would do that."

Dan was thoughtful for a minute, then said, "That is very interesting, Saphet. Aksu told me he noticed some red smears on the basket. Did you see them?"

"I did. They appeared to be fresh paint, still wet."

Suddenly his eyes opened wide, "I thought it was paint. It could have been blood!"

Dan said, "We need to find that basket."

Kathleen folded her arms, "And just how do you propose to do that?"

Dan frowned. "I don't know." Then he asked Saphet, "Did you tell this to the police?"

Now Saphet frowned, "The police? No, I never talked to them, they never talked to me, I mean."

"Of course they didn't. The police didn't know about Aksu, or you." Then Dan turned to Aksu, "If you live with your great uncle, you must have a key to his house, right?"

"Yes," said the youngster.

"Then let's take a look at the house. Thank you, Saphet. I doubt the police would be interested in your story, but it wouldn't hurt to tell them if you want."

"Not me," said Saphet, "I don't want to get involved." Then he hastened back to his shop.

"Okay, then. We should try to find your uncle, Aksu, why don't you go with me and Kathleen to your house? Perhaps we can find a clue there that will lead us to him. We need a taxi, where's the phone?"

Saphet Sadat, Nekhtou's neighbor, the rug merchant, was indeed a distant relative of Anwar Sadat, third president of Egypt, who was killed in a coup in 1981. A distant cousin twice removed, or somethin like that.

"I am no fool," thought Saphet. *"I know human sweat and I know blood when I smell it. I know Nekhtou killed that young man that came to his shop, an American. I saw him go in, and I helped carry him out in that basket, and I am certain Nekhtou took his body out to the desert to dispose of it. I know he has been selling things brought to him to that other American in the seersucker suit for years. I am sure much of it was illegal. He lives in that fancy house, but I live in an apartment."* He thought much about Nekhtou's lucrative business and envied his success.

Chapter 8

SOMETHING BIG

When their taxi arrived at the address in a very upscale neighborhood, Dan was surprised to see the house was large and quite modern. There was a Mercedes in the driveway. This old codger who had a small jewelry shop in the bazaar was very well off, though he didn't look wealthy. And Aksu was not the dirty little urchin he first appeared to be. The house was two stories and a small, attractive wall surrounded it. There were palm trees and green shrubbery distributed in places around the stylish house.

When Aksu saw the car, he shouted, "Uncle Nekhtou is here! That is his car."

The taxi had barely stopped when Aksu leaped out and ran for the front door. Dan asked the driver to wait, handing him a

$10.00 bill, then he and Kathleen casually walked to the door that Aksu had left ajar after letting himself in with his key. Dan rapped loudly on the door, and shouted, "Hello," then ushered Kathleen in ahead of him. They were met by Nekhtou and Aksu. Again, Dan and Kathleen were astounded at the sumptuous furnishings inside, something like an old Hollywood movie.

"Uncle Nekhtou, these are my new friends. They were going to help me find you."

Dan stuck out his hand and said, "I'm Good. Dan Good, and this is my wife, Kathleen."

Nekhtou did not shake hands, but bowed, "Welcome to our humble home. I am Nekhtou Gamal."

Dan noticed that Nekhtou's hair was wet and his clothes looked fresh.

"I hope we are not intruding."

"Not at all," said Nekhtou, "I was just getting myself refreshed after my last delivery."

"Aksu was worried about you being away from your shop so long. The Cairo Police evidently found it opened and abandoned and believed you had been robbed and possibly harmed."

"Aksu is a very good boy. I called the police and talked with them as soon as I got home. I had an urgent delivery today."

"What could have caused it to be so urgent, if I may ask?"

"It is a private business matter."

Dan wanted very much to ask about the red smears on the basket but knew it would do no good to ask. Nekhtou was being quit secretive. He got a tingling in the back of his neck, and thought, *"There is something afoot."*

"You have a very lovely home," said Kathleen.

"Thank you mam," then, turning to Aksu, he said, "Go get a bath and put on clean clothes, Aksu." Then, he turned back to Dan and Kathleen, "Please, be seated, and we will visit a while as Aksu gets cleaned up. Egypt is very sandy, as you well know by now. He gets very dirty playing with the other children at the bazaar"

Dan seated Kathleen on a plush light blue sofa, then sat beside her.

"Could I get you some refreshments, a drink, perhaps? I have Coca-Cola or iced tea."

"Don't feel you have to entertain us; we have a cab waiting, we must not stay long. We would enjoy taking you and Aksu to dinner at our hotel later tonight."

"No, thank you. I already have a supper engagement tonight," said Nekhtou, "I thank you for befriending Aksu while I was away. Have you been enjoying you visit to my country?"

"It has not only been fascinating, but awesome," said Kathleen. Just then, they heard the sound of Aksu running out of the bathroom, down the stairs and into the livingroom. "Uncle Nekhtou, how do I look?"

"You look very well dressed, Aksu. Thank you for being so fast."

"You are a very handsome young man," said Kathleen.

The boy beamed and threw out his little chest. "Thank you, mam." He went to Kathleen and squeezed in to sit beside her. She readily helped him and put her arm around his small body. They both appeared to enjoy their comradery immensely. Dan smiled at them, then stood and turned to the old man.

"I'm sure you need to rest, I think it is time we left, sir."

Nekhtou stood and bowed slightly. "As you wish. It has been our pleasure to meet you and have you in our home, hasn't it Aksu."

The boy also jumped up. "Oh, yes! I wish you wouldn't go."

"You must not interfere with the plans of these new friends of ours, Aksu," then to Dan and Kathleen, he said, "Please, come again sometime."

"Thank you for your kind hospitality."

As Dan and Kathleen went to their waiting taxi, Kathleen said softly, "Did you smell that strong odor of bleach?"

"I did. And I saw no signs of a woman. Where was his wife and Aksu's mother?"

"It is strange. Bleach is good for cleaning up blood, you know."

"Circumstantial, sweetheart, but quite possible. I also think the old man is not nearly as ancient as he appears. He is quite agile."

After they were settled in the taxi, Kathleen asked, "But Dan, how can he afford to live in such a large house filled with expensive furnishings? I understand most people in Cairo live in apartments, only the very wealthy can afford houses. Surely his small shop doesn't bring in that kind of wealth even if he is selling jewelry," said Kathleen.

"Good point, sweetheart. He must have a secondary income, and it could be something nefarious. I intend to continue a little more sleuthing. I sense something big is going on."

"What are you thinking, honey?"

"I'm thinking Nekhtou may have killed that young college student. I need to learn all I can about our friend, Nekhtou Gamal. I want to talk to his neighbors."

"But," said Kathleen, "You can't do that tomorrow, remember. Muslim's don't work on Fridays, it's their day for worship."

"You're right about tomorrow; perhaps Saturday."

"So, what can you do tomorrow?"

"I'm thinking, I'm thinking," said Dan.

After the taxi drove away with Dan and Kathleen, Nekhtou sent Aksu outside to play, and walked over to a front window. The taxi was long gone, but he stared out the window, thinking, *Cursed Americans! Death to the infidels!"*

His wife, Cliupatra, had slipped silently down the stairs to stand beside him. "They are gone," she said softly in Masri (an Egyptian Arabic dialect).

Nekhtou turned toward his wife, also speaking Masri. "Yes, tell Jomana that she may come down now. I have something to tell you both."

She quietly went back upstairs immediately, and in moments returned with Jomana. Both women were dressed in Abayas as Muslim women were required, though none of them were actually practicing Muslims. The ladies sat side by side on the couch. Nekhtou stood before them.

"We will soon move to America," he announced.

Both women smiled with delight, eyes shining. Cliupatra clapped her hands one time and said enthusiastically, "At long last!"

"You may start now to prepare for this move. I have chosen Texas as the state in America because I've heard that much of it desert and it is warm. Not too unlike Cairo, I think. I believe we would be very comfortable there."

"Oh Nekhtou, this is such wonderful news, thank you, my husband. And Jomana and Aksu will be most happy there too."

"Oh, yes, uncle Nekhtou," said Jomana. She and Aksu were living with Cliupatra and Nekhtou because Jomana was a young widow.

"Good," said Nekhtou, "I knew you would be pleased. However, I must go to a very important business supper tonight. I do not know what time I should be home."

Then he frowned and said, "Never say anything of my need to cleanse myself this afternoon upon my return from my work. It was an unfortunate incident. You understand?"

"Of course, my husband. Not a word, as always."

Chapter 9

PARTNERS IN CRIME

Egyptians eat at times of the day that are quite different than Americans. Most eat only two meals a day. Their main meal is between two and three in the afternoon, then a much lighter meal between nine and ten p.m. But Dan and Kathleen maintained their American eating times.

"It's almost six, honey," said Dan, "where would you like to go for dinner tonight?"

"El Fenix sounds good to me," said Kathleen.

"That is a bit far, you know."

"Just longing. Why don't we go somewhere we haven't been before?"

"I heard someone mention a pizza place called Maison Thomas."

"That sounds more like home. I love pizza."

"Are you getting homesick, sweetheart? We can go anytime you wish."

"Oh, no. Not yet, I'm just hungry for something like we eat in Dallas.

"Okay, Maison Thomas it is," said Dan as he picked up the phone. I'll call us a cab."

The Maison Thomas is an Italian cuisine in Cairo, located at 157 26 of July St. Zamalek. It is a small eatery, but it was packed when Dan and Kathleen got out of their cab. Their wait was not long. Just fifteen minutes or so, and they were seated at a table near the back.

"Oh, Dan, the aroma is wonderful. Thank you for finding this place. I know I'll love the pizza."

While waiting for their food, Kathleen leaned near Dan to whisper, "Did you see that man who just came in? He is sitting at the bar. The man in the dirty, rumpled seersucker suit. He looks like a troublemaker to me."

Dan looked at him, "He looks like some kind of professor to me," he countered. "Did you notice the nice attaché he has?"

"A professor? You're kidding me. He looks like a tramp."

Just then their pizza came, and they dug in, forgetting about the man at the bar. In a very few minutes, Dan noticed the man at the bar was moving to a table just behind Kathleen. He had a pizza and a beer.

Dan leaned to whisper to Kathleen, "Don't look, but your tramp just moved to the table right behind you. He brought a nice pizza and a beer with him."

Kathleen's eye widened a little, but she said, "Today was wonderful sweetie, I really am enjoying our honeymoon."

"I'm very glad, honey. It is so nice for us to be together."

As Dan was speaking to Kathleen, he glanced to lock eyes briefly with the man at the table behind her, and he smiled back at Dan. Then, he suddenly stood, lifted his plate, and picked up his beer. He brought his meal to their table, and said, "I heard your Texas accents, and thought we Texans should meet. Mind if I join you?"

Dan stood, "Not at all. We are glad to find another fellow Texan in Cairo. I'm Good, Dan Good, and this is my wife, Kathleen. We met another Texan just yesterday."

"Really," said their visitor, "I'm Professor Wilson Webber, but you can call me Will."

Dan and Will sat down, and Dan saw Kathleen's surprised look on her face. He smiled at her.

"You said you met another Texan," said Will, "it wouldn't be by any chance, Justin Case, would it?"

"Yes, do you know him, too?"

"Oh, yes, quite well. We are business associates."

"Business associates? I thought you said you were a professor," said Kathleen. "You aren't a broker of Egyptian antiquities as well, are you?"

"I am. Guilty as charged. Mostly scarabs."

Dan and Kathleen exchanged glances.

Dan cleared his throat and said, "Would you, by any chance, be selling him the Ramses scarab?"

"Oh. You know about that scarab?"

"We had lunch with Justin yesterday. He told us about the Ramses scarab, and that he was going to buy it from his broker soon."

"That is very interesting that we have these connections. Now there are four of us Texans in Cairo, plus my six students, though only one of them is really a Texan." Will chuckled. "I wonder if there are others."

"I don't know of any, but who knows?" said Dan. "Where and what do you teach, professor?"

"Please, just call me Will. I teach archeology at Texas University in Austin."

Kathleen spoke, "We plan to invite Justin for dinner with us tomorrow tonight, we would love for you to join us. I think it might be fun, don't you, sweetheart?"

"Of course. We would be happy for you to join us, Will," said Dan.

"Oh, I'm sorry," said Will, "I have an

appointment that prevents me. Perhaps another time?"

"Certainly," said Dan.

Kathleen asked, "Do you broker other antiquities, Will?"

"No, not really," said Will. "Most Egyptian antiquities are controlled by the Egyptian government now. Scarabs are so plentiful in Egypt they are about the only things I can dabble with as a broker."

When the three of them were done eating, they made their goodbyes and went their separate ways.

On their way back to their hotel in their taxi, Kathleen said thoughtfully, "What did you think of our newfound friend from Texas? And how did you know he was a professor?"

"I didn't know he was a professor, I just thought he could be. But I am a little perplexed about him and Justin."

"Perplexed? Why, sweetheart?"

"For example, I know just how much the Egyptian government controls their antiquities now. There was a time when England sort of ravaged them at will, as did America and other countries. I also have learned since we came here that scarabs are available by the thousands, but I believe the government here probably protects the more expensive scarabs, especially like the Ramses scarab. It is a great Egyptian treasure. I can't see how our professor can broker the sale of it. Surely the Egyptian government would not let such a treasure leave their country in the hands of a private American if they knew of it. I think it's all illegal. I believe Will and Justin are stealing the Ramses scarab from right under the Egyptian Government's nose. They are partners in crime."

Kathleen was stunned. "The Egyptian government knows nothing at all about the Ramses scarab? Oh, Dan, what are we to do?"

Dan waited till they were back in their hotel room to explain the situation more fully to Kathleen.

"First of all, honey," he said, "we can't go to the Egyptian authorities to tell them what's going on."

"Why not?"

"We have nothing to tell them. If we told the authorities what we know and they questioned Will and Justin, all they need do is deny knowing anything about it. We haven't seen the scarab. We have no proof it even exists, much less that it's been found."

Kathleen was bewildered.

"Then, what can we do?"

"I will just have to figure things out myself."

"So we're having a working honeymoon, unofficially."

"I'm sorry, sweetheart, but I see no other way. What our new friends are doing is illegal, and they must be exposed and stopped."

"I'm not complaining, I know you are right, and I know you are just the man for the job. Do what you have to do but let me tag along like last time."

He took her in his arms, and said, "You'll do much more than just tag along." Then he kissed her.

Chapter 10

IF AT FIRST...

Tuesday morning, June 11, 1985, Cairo, Egypt.

The phone rang on the bedside table next to Dan. He roused from a deep sleep, looked at his clock and saw it was nine a.m. Then he grabbed the receiver and answered, "Hello?"

"Good morning Dan, I'm sorry to bother you on your honeymoon." Dan recognized Walter Ellis' voice immediately.

"Good morning, Walter," said Dan as he swung his feet on to the floor and sat up on the side of the bed. Kathleen roused, turned and lifted herself on to her elbow.

"Who is it, honey?"

Dan whispered, "It's Walter." Then, into the phone said, "Not a problem, Walter, what's up?"

"Have you heard about a murder yesterday?"

"A murder? Where, here in Cairo? No, who?"

"A young college student of archaeology from Princeton University there on a dig. His name was Jacob Isaac."

"No, not Paul Isaac's son?"

"Yes indeed, and Paul has stirred a hornet's nest; Princeton is outraged that one of their top students was murdered. President Reagan has called us in on the investigation, and the press has gone wild. The whole of DC is aroused. Instead of sending a man to Cairo, though, I want to hire you, as a freelancer, to investigate for us."

"Me? I'm on my honeymoon."

"I know, but we really need to jump on this case as soon as possible, and you are already there. Couldn't you nose around a bit for us? I'll have to get a few things all sorted out for you. I'll have to have a talk to Hosni Mubarak, first."

Dan didn't have to think long, and said, "Okay, Walter, I will. I had already decided to do some sleuthing on my own about another matter. This will allow me to do it legally."

"Fine. I knew we could count on you. Thanks."

"Not a problem, you're welcome. Oh, before we hang up, how are Donna and the kids?"

"Mayhem, chaos, confusion and havoc. Everything is normal in the Ellis household."

They both chuckled as they hung up. Dan turned to Kathleen and said, "You heard?"

"Paul Isaac's son was murdered? When? Where?

"Out in the desert somewhere near Luxor, yesterday. He was here on a dig."

"NO! So, we are *officially* interrupting our honeymoon now."

"I'm sorry, sweetheart, but I don't think this will take long."

"Of course I understand, honey. Just giving you a hard time. No one is better than you."

"I know you don't want to just sit around on your thumbs on our honeymoon. We'll make another adventure for us out of this."

They kissed, and Dan said, "I want to go down to Police Headquarters, but I'm in no hurry. Walter has to get things all sorted out for me. I will wait until after lunch, I think."

"Good," said Kathleen as she raised up and wrapped her arms around his neck.

Murders in Cairo were not uncommon, as the rate for the 1980s thus far varied between around 50 to around 80 a year. But the murder of an American college student from Princeton University on a dig was quite uncommon. The Cairo police force would feel great pressure from many American sources, like the American Embassy, Princeton University, the young man's parents, Washington, DC, the American press and more, to solve this murder. The Cairo police department was in a frenzy, and the murder of Jacob Isaac quickly leaked to the general public, and distorted rumors spread like wildfire.

It was about 1:30 when Dan entered the Cairo Police Headquarters building. It was a large building with columns along the front.

Inside, it was like a Chinese fire drill. Cops were running about and shouting in Masri. Regular cops in white uniforms with funny little black caps.

"They all look like flatheads in those caps," thought Dan. He also saw many in Muslim garb, and some in suits. These, he assumed, were detectives. He stopped a passing uniform, "Pardon, me. Do you speak English?"

The young man frowned at him, "Yes, of course. Who are you, and what are you doing in here?"

"I need to speak to your Chief of Police."

The young man's frown deepened, "Chief? We have no chief; I think you mean our Lieutenant General." Then he pointed toward the rear of the enormous room to a closed door.

"There," he said, and quickly went away.

Dan walked casually to the door and knocked. A uniformed cop opened the door, suddenly startled at Dan's six-nine frame. All sound stopped as Dan entered and shut the door behind him. "I'm here to see your Lieutenant General of Police."

A booming voice erupted, speaking English, "Everybody out, except our visitor, and Lieutenant General Mostafa."

The exit was immediate, and Dan looked at two men in what was obviously high-ranking uniforms.

"Do sit down. I'm sure you must be Dan Good, a representative from the United States Government."

"Yes, thank you," and he sat in a chair across a large desk from a big heavy Egyptian. The other man took a seat next to the desk, but the man behind the desk remained standing. Dan knew *he* was in charge.

He said, "I am Lieutenant General Oman of the Cairo Police department." He waved a heavy hand toward the seated man by his desk. "This is Lieutenant General Mostafa of Egypt's National Police. We have joined in the investigation of the murder of your country's visiting student. A tragic thing, I am sorry."

In a voice, damaged by smoking, the other man spoke gruffly and rasping, "We are quite capable of handling our crimes in Egypt, and I, for one, deeply resent your interference in our business."

Dan responded, "I'm certain you are, sir, but I have an assignment from my government."

The one named Oman spoke up. "Of course you do, Mr. Good, we have been expecting you. We are currently making preparations for a general briefing of our people. It will begin at eight a.m. tomorrow morning. You are most welcome to attend if you wish."

"Fine," said Dan. "I will be as unobtrusive as I can and will be present and on time tomorrow. Thank you, gentlemen." He stood to leave.

Neither man moved to shake hands and they said, almost in unison, "Goodbye Mr. Good."

After Dan had left Police Headquarters, the two Lieutenant Generals looked at each other.

Lieutenant General Oman said, "What can we do about our Mr. Good?"

"American pig. We don't need him butting in on our investigation."

"I know, but what choice do we have?"

Lieutenant General Mostafa smiled. "I have an idea."

It was almost noon when Dan returned, and when he entered their suite, Kathleen was dressed to go out for lunch. She said, "How about Chinese, honey?"

"Sounds great to me," said Dan, "whatever you wish, sweetheart.

"I found one called '8 Chinese,' and made us a reservation."

"Did you get the address?"

"Of course. It's 1089 Corniche El Nile in Garden City."

"Okay, let me get ready. I need to wash up."

When they got to the restaurant, their table was in a private room overlooking the Nile.

"This is so beautiful, Dan. That was a lovely waterfall fixture in the entrance. The soft music and the sound of water flowing is wonderful ambiance. It is so romantic, sweetheart, I love it."

"It is very nice. The view is terrific."

Kathleen ordered a lite meal, but Dan's selection, when it came, was larger than he expected.

"Don't know if I can eat all this, but it is delicious," he said after taking a bite. "Glad you found this place, honey."

She said, "How did your visit to Police Headquarters go this morning?"

"It didn't go so well."

"Really?"

"No, they resented me butting in on their murder investigation."

"Didn't Walter request you to them?"

"Oh, yes, and President Hosni Mubarak as well, but they didn't like it."

"I'm surprised. I thought they would be happy for your help, after all you have a great reputation in the States, don't they know that?"

"Perhaps, but they were very unhappy to see me. However, I *was* invited to attend their briefing tomorrow morning. I hope I will learn what they know about the murder."

"You plan to go?"

"Sure, 'If at first…'"

"'… you don't succeed, keep on sucking till you do succeed…' I know, but I think you will be wasting your time."

Chapter 11

THE CURSE CONTINUES

They met at the Koshari al-Tahrir
restaurant in downtown Cairo at nine p.m.
sharp.

"You brought the money?"

"Of course not. Did you bring the
scarab?"

"Certainly not."

They nodded to each other and went
inside. They were seated at a table by a
window. "I've already had my dinner," said
Webber. "You Egyptians eat at crazy times."

Nekhtou picked up a menu. "I am
famished. Our business can wait till I am
finished enjoying a good Egyptian meal."

Nekhtou didn't take long to make his
choice. Webber ordered a beer, and the
waiter left. Neither man trusted the other
though they'd been doing business for
nearly five years. Their purpose tonight was

to work out the final details of how and when the exchange could be safely achieved. In spite of what he'd said about waiting, Nekhtou said, "While we are waiting for my food, tell me you really have a million dollars in cash."

"I do. Why do you want to know?"

"I've never seen that much money. I don't know what to expect."

"Of course I have already taken my finder's fee out of it, so it's not quite a million we are talking about. I have your money out in my car."

Nekhtou raised his eyebrows, "Really? It is so much money."

Webber smiled, "Just what do you plan to do with so much money, beside paying the original finder his fee?"

A cold calm seemed to settle over Nekhtou, and he looked at Webber with dead eyes. "The finder has already received his fee, all of it will be mine."

"Yeah, right."

Nekhtou's meal came and he began eating. Webber ordered another beer. When Nekhtou's plates were cleared and his teacup refilled, he looked into his cup as he took his first sip, and said, "Let's get this done."

"Fine. How, when, and where?

"I believe you said you have the money in your rental car. I have the scarab in my car. We can make the trade out on the sidewalk on the crowded street. No one will pay any attention to us but would notice any violence should it occur."

"An interesting idea, my friend."

"We are not friends. We are businessmen."

"Indeed," said Webber.

"Just let me finish my tea."

Webber made a peevish face, but Nekhtou finished off his karkaday quickly. He was anxious to do the deed.

Nekhtou never noticed that Saphet, his bazaar neighbor, was seated in a far corner of the restaurant at a small table. He had followed Nekhtou and slipped inside as he and Webber were sitting down, and watched them carefully, wondering about what they were talking about.

When they went outside, Webber and Nekhtou each went to his car, then came together on the sidewalk face to face.

"I'll show you mine if you show me yours," said Webber grinning.

Nekhtou was holding the scarab with all the documents in a soft cloth sack. He held it close to his body. Webber set the case of cash on the sidewalk between them. Nekhtou handed the cloth bag to Webber and picked up the case. They each turned to walk to their respective cars.

When Nekhtou had put the money in the trunk of his car, he quickly went to the driver's seat. He would count it later, there was just too much to count now. He wanted to get away as fast as he could. As he started to put the key in the ignition there was a sudden soft cough sounding in his ear. The front of his head exploded.

Webber quickly surveyed his surroundings. The noisy crowds in the street had not heard the silenced shot, nor even looked in his direction. They didn't notice what had happened at all. Webber was glad for the silencer on his Glock. There was only blank paper in the case in Nekhtou's trunk, but he wanted to keep his case. He was very much afraid of the curse, so he quickly retrieved it and walked briskly back to his car and drove away.

The curse had continued.

Saphet, however, was watching the entire transaction and had seen everything. Webber didn't notice him at all. He was just another person among the pedestrians on the street. Saphet walked casually to his own car, and sat for a while, thinking about what he'd seen. He was sure Webber now had the Ramses scarab, so he decided to keep a close eye on Webber.

Webber parked his rental car a half a block from the Ritz-Carlton Hotel and quickly carried the big cloth bag up to Justin Case's rooms on the fifth floor. He knocked, and Case opened the door. "You have the scarab?"

"I do. And the documents."

"Come in, come in, please professor."

He quickly walked in. It was obvious Webber was very nervous. "You have the cash?"

"Certainly," said Case. "It is in that case by the coffee table. Would you like to stay a while and have coffee?"

"No. I want this done now."

"Fine. Set the sack down, please, I want to look everything over. I'm not giving you a penny until I am certain of my purchase. You go count the money."

Webber crossed to the coffee table, sat on the couch, pulled the bag close to him, opened it, and began counting the money.

Case opened the sack near the small table for eating in his rooms. The first thing he took out was the Ramses scarab. He took it out of the soft cloth it was wrapped in, laid it on the table before him, and began examining it intensely.

It was truly beautiful to behold. It was indeed six inches long, but it was carved in great detail; the head showed every nuance of structure, the body as well. It was solid gold, but two small sapphires were set in the head for its eyes: deep blue-black eyes. The wings were also carefully carved, and there were nice sized diamonds, emeralds, rubies, and amethysts on its back. One diamond, the one in the center of the back, was very large. The back also had also been delicately carved in great detail, and there were some tiny hieroglyphics carved along its sides. Of course, Case did not read hieroglyphics. The scarab also had legs and antenna added by some hard, material in such a manner they could not be broken off easily, though they were somewhat thin. The beetle was clearly defined.

Case sat for some time absorbing the object in his mind, admiring its great beauty. Then he took all the parchments out, but of course, they too were in hieroglyphics. He'd expected them to be in English. *"How stupid of me,"* he thought. Just because Webber quoted them in English, he'd made a false assumption. He wondered if Webber had someone translate it for him, or whether Webber could read hieroglyphics.

Thinking of Webber made him turn to look at him, but he was gone. He'd taken the money and left. Case had not heard him leave; he was too absorbed in looking at the scarab. Webber never said, "Thank you," or "goodbye." Well, he thought, neither did I. Suddenly, he wondered if Webber might die soon.

Saphet had followed Webber up to Justin Case's suite, unnoticed. He lingered in the hallway until Webber came out and left. Webber didn't notice a man in the hall. Saphet quickly followed him at a discrete distance, but now he knew the Ramses scarab was in that room. Webber had come out with a large case, probably full of money. The man in that suite had bought the Ramses scarab. There was likely very nearly a million dollars in that case. He thought for a moment about killing Webber and taking the money, but he had become obsessed with the scarab. It was the scarab he wanted most. Now, he also wanted to kill Webber for the money, but he'd never killed before, and wasn't sure he could. He decided he would just continue watching both Webber and the man in the suite. Who was the man in the suite? Saphet had a few friends that worked in the hotel. He could get his name and whatever else he wanted.

Chapter 12

THE ARRANGEMENT

Wednesday morning, June 12, 1985, Cairo, Egypt.

It was midnight when Nekhtou's body was found in his car, but the Cairo Police waited till morning to go tell his family.

Two Homicide Detectives knocked firmly on the front door at eight a.m. Cliupatra took her time, making sure she was properly dressed in her Abaya as a Muslim woman should be before going downstairs. She went to the door and opened it.

"Yes?"

"Police, Mrs. Gamal. I am Detective Oshe." Then he introduced his partner, Detective Husani. "We have an urgent matter to speak to you about, may we come in?"

They held their badges up for her to inspect them. Cliupatra frowned in sudden alarm, but stepped back to let the policemen in. "Yes, of course," she said, "Come in, please."

She waved a hand toward their plush light blue sofa. "Please sit. Jomana," she called to her niece, "Please bring tea for three."

In moments, Jomana appeared with a tray, set it on the large coffee table and left. Cliupatra served the men, then herself, and sat opposite them in a large wing chair. "What has happened? Is it my husband?"

"Yes," said Detective Oshe, "I'm very sorry to tell you your husband is dead." The Detectives ignored their tea.

Cliupatra's composure never changed. Calmly, she set her cup on a side table by her chair, and asked, "How did it happen?"

Detective Oshe looked at her keenly for any emotion but saw none. "I am so sorry to tell you, he was murdered."

Suddenly, Cliupatra was startled. Her eyebrows went up, her eyes widened. "Nekhtou was in very poor heath, so I have prepared myself for his death, but Murder? No! How did it happen? Where is he. May I see him?"

"He was shot, but we must perform an autopsy before you can see him."

"I quite understand Detective. Do you know who shot him?"

"No, we found him dead in his car sometime after he was shot."

"Will you find his killer?"

"Oh, yes," said detective Oshe with unwarranted confidence. "We will find his killer, I assure you."

"Thank you for coming to tell me, Detectives. Is there anything more you can tell me?"

"I am afraid not, sorry. We must go now."

After they left, Jomana darted into the room, "Oh, Cliupatra! I listened. What are we to do? Will we still move to America?"

"No, Jomana, I am sure there is not enough money now. I believe Nekhtou was killed for the money, the old fool. Unfortunately, he never told me much of anything about his side business, but it seems I now have a small jewelry shop to run in the bazaar. It is our only means of survival now. I must get ready to open the shop today. We are going to need every pound we can make now. I'm going to change clothes and go to our shop. You stay here with Aksu, and care for our house."

"No, Cliupatra, I must help you in the shop. Aksu can go to the shop with us as he did with Nekhtou."

"Yes. That is a good idea. You are right. Together, you and I, we can do a better job, and make more money. Let's get ready and go to our new business, Jomana, but we can dress in western wear, no Abayas anymore. We are *not* Muslims."

At the same time the detectives came to tell Cliupatra of her husband's murder, Dan Good entered Police Headquarters in downtown Cairo. In fact, Dan was a little early. He found out where the briefing would take place, and hurried so he would not be late. It was a corner room in the building, and large. He was surprised to see so many cops, some in their white uniforms, some in Muslim attire, and some in business suites. Lieutenant General Oman was standing at a podium, Mustafa was seated behind him. The room was full. Every seat was taken, so Dan sidled to the back of the room to sit precariously perched on a narrow windowsill. It was uncomfortable, but what else could he do? He noticed a large chalkboard behind Oman and on either side were bulletin boards covered with photos and notices of various sizes, all in Masri. All the writing on the chalkboard was also in Masri. Then, as Oman began the briefing, he spoke only in Masri. Dan realized no one had greeted him or welcomed him. It was obvious Kathleen had been right, it was a waste of time for him to come. He was being excluded, but instead of making a fuss about it, Dan decided he would just quietly slip out the door.

When the two ladies arrived at Nekhtou's shop and went inside, Cliupatra looked around at the mess the police had left when they searched it, thinking the shop had been robbed.

" Just look at this mess, Jomana, the police must have done this."

"This will take us some time before we can open for business, Cliupatra."

They sent Aksu out to play, and without another word, the women went to work. It took them two hours, but they not only had things in order, they had completely renovated the little jewelry shop, making it neater, more presentable, and functional. They stopped and stood, surveying what they had done.

"Oh, Cliupatra, this is so nice and pretty."

Cliupatra was bursting with pride. She fully believed the little shop would now draw more customers just because it looked so nice and colorful.

"All it needed was a woman's touch, Jomana. Let's get this place open for business."

Cliupatra had been right, the business thrived with the two pretty women running the shop.

There was a line of customers at Nekhtou's little jewelry shop when Kathleen got there, so she got in the queue. She waited her turn patiently. When it was her turn, she said, "Mrs. Gamal? My name is Kathleen Good. My husband and I came by yesterday and your husband showed us a nice scarab. I came as quickly as I could. Is he here? I want to buy it. Your husband said the price was $900.00 American. Is it still available, or have you sold it?"

The price got her attention. "My husband is dead, Mrs. Good. He was murdered last night. Let me look for that scarab for you." She went back inside, and in a few minutes, returned with a small tray of quality scarabs. Of course, Kathleen and Dan already bought it, but Kathleen looked for the best she could find, and pretended she had found what she asked for. "This is it! You will still accept American Express?"

"Yes, mam," said Cliupatra.

After her purchase, and as she turned to leave, Kathleen turned back and said, "I'm so sorry for your loss, Mrs. Gamal, and, by the way, we know what your husband did, we actually *knew* the young man he killed, and I believe we know why your husband was killed and by whom." Then she walked quickly away.

Cliupatra turned to Jomana and said, "Oh, Jomana, did you hear what that woman said to me?"

"I did, but I don't understand."

"I don't understand either, but she really frightened me. She said Nekhtou killed someone, and she knew who killed Nekhtou and why. She really scared me. I don't know what to do."

Jomana replied, "I think you must go to the police."

"The police? I can't go to the police! Let's go home, *now*! Call Aksu in."

Jomana stepped outside, and just as Cliupatra had shooed away her last customer and was shutting the store, a man suddenly appeared, calling her name. She turned to see a tall man in a rumpled seersucker suit. "We are closed," she told him.

"I know, but I want to give you some money I owed Nekhtou."

"Nekhtou is dead," she said.

"I know that, too, but I thought you should have his finder's fee. I sold a scarab for him to a rich American and thought you should get his finder's fee."

Cliupatra eyed Webber warily, "I have seen you in our shop before, but I don't know you. I think you are an evil man. I don't want to have anything to do with you. Now go away."

"I'm sorry you feel that way," Webber smiled, "let me introduce myself. I'm Professor Webber from the University of Texas, and I'm here because I had a business arrangement with your husband. Just take a quick look in this envelope. There is five thousand dollars in it. Please."

Cautiously, Cliupatra took the envelope and opened it. She had never seen that much cash before in her life. Her eyes went wide. "I... I don't know what to say."

"It is yours to keep and do with as you want." To Webber, five thousand dollars was not much out of his million dollars. It was cheap enough to get Cliupatra to form a business agreement like he had with Nekhtou. "I would like to make an arrangement with you like I had with your husband."

Cliupatra did not want to let go of her fortune and reconsidered. "Alright," she said. "But only on a trial basis. We will see about more afterward."

"Great. Thanks. I think you will enjoy the extra side money from your jewelry shop. Nekhtou made much more doing business with me than from his shop."

After Webber left, Cliupatra showed Jomana the money and told her about the arrangement with Webber.

"He is a university professor from Texas, where Nekhtou wanted us to move to. I still don't like him any more than rotting fish."

"Oh, but, Cliupatra, so much money, and it is tax free."

"I am very upset, Jomana. I am too upset to work anymore today. Let's go home."

Chapter 13

A LITTLE BONE RATTLING

When Kathleen got back to the hotel, Dan was there. "Hi, sweetheart," said Kathleen. "Have you been waiting long?"

"Not long, where did you go?"

"I ran down to Nekhtou's shop for a minute. Nekhtou was murdered last night. His wife was running the shop with, I guess, Aksu's mother."

"Yeah? I guess it's her shop now. Too bad about Nekhtou. That is two murders now over that scarab."

"I know. And I bought another scarab."

"You did?" Why? You thinking of becoming a collector too?"

"Oh, no. I pretended we didn't buy the scarab from Nekhtou, and I had come back for it. I found one that looked similar to the one in the safe downstairs, and I bought it and dropped this new one off in the safe with the other one before coming up."

"Okay, tell me about it, sweetie."

"Just as I was leaving, I turned back to tell her we knew her husband had murdered that student, and we knew who killed Nekhtou and why. I think it shook her up."

Dan laughed, "I'm sure it did. That gives me an idea. Would it be alright with you if we invited Justin to lunch with us?"

"Sure, why not?"

Dan went to the nearest phone and dialed. When he answered, Dan said, "Justin, this is Dan Good. Kathleen and I would like to invite you to lunch with us."

""How very nice of you. I am delighted, yes. Do you want to meet upstairs?"

"Yes, we are headed that way now, if that is alright with you."

"I'll meet you there." And he hung up.

"He's coming," said Dan, "I'm ready when you are."

"If you're waiting on me, your boots are on backwards."

They laughed together as they left.

At the restaurant, Justin had arrived first, but was still at the entrance.

Kathleen said, "It is such a lovely day, why don't we eat on the terrace?"

Dan smiled at her, "As you wish, my dear."

Soon they were all three seated and had ordered. "I think it somewhat unusual for newlyweds to invite a third wheel for lunch, so I suspect you have a matter you want to discuss with me. Right?"

Dan looked intently at Justin and said, "You are correct, sir. I want to talk to you about your Ramses scarab."

"Oh?"

"Yes. Justin, I know the Egyptian Government has been robbed of its great treasures for a very long time as several countries came here and pillaged this land, taking marvelous artifacts back to their homelands to put them in their museums. But, not long ago, the Egyptian Government put a stop to that. They no longer allow their great treasures to be confiscated."

Justin nodded, "I know that."

"Well, I also now know that scarabs are still quite plentiful, and people all over the world collect them. The Egyptian Government allows this. But *your* Ramses scarab is not just another scarab, it is of a value, beyond imagination."

Justin sat up straighter in his chair, "Just what are you getting at?"

"I think you know. I believe that if the Egyptian Government knew about it, they would never allow it to leave their land.

They would proudly display it in the Cairo Museum."

"What do you know about anything? Who are you to interfere in my business? That scarab is *mine!* I paid for it."

"But, I think what you and Webber have done is illegal. If the Government knew what you and your professor friend have done, you would both be arrested. I think you should give it back to its rightful owners."

Justin suddenly stood, "No! It's *mine!* They know nothing about it. I will *not* give it to them. Stay out of my business." He strode resolutely out of the restaurant, in a rage.

"That went over like the proverbial led balloon," said Kathleen.

"Just about as I expected," said Dan. "The man is obsessed."

"What's next, cutie?"

"After lunch, let's see if we can find Mr. Webber. I want to talk to the professor."

"Webber? Why?"

"I want to rattle his bones, too."

"Rattle his bones? Where did you get that idea?"

"From you, sweetheart," said Dan.

"From me?"

"You started it, pumpkin."

"I started it?"

"You sure are full of questions. Of course you started it when you visited

Nekhtou's wife and niece and rattled their bones. A great idea, honey. Brilliant. I'm very proud of you. We'll rattle all their bones and see what fall out. I'm going to try to find Webber."

"How can you find him? Cairo is a big city; he could be anywhere."

"When we get back to our suite, I have Justin's number. I'm sure he has Webber's."

They enjoyed a nice lunch and went back down to their suite. Dan went straight to the phone and dialed. When Dan heard Justin answer, he said, "Justin? I need Will Webber's phone number, please," he put his hand over the mouthpiece and said to Kathleen, "You get better results if you say 'Please.'"

"Mr. Good? I don't want to give you his phone number."

"Don't hang up. If you don't give it to me, I know your room number, and I'll come up there and wring your neck till you give it to me... understand?"

"With a shaky voice, Justin said, "Alright, alright," and he gave him Webber's number.

Dan committed it to memory and said, "Thank you Justin," but he'd already slammed the phone down in anger.

Dan smiled, and gently laid the receiver in the cradle, "Rattled his bones again, I did."

Kathleen laughed, "You're amazing. I guess 'please' didn't work this time."

Dan grinned and dialed Webber's number. He was surprised when Webber answered.

"Hello, Will. Wasn't sure you would be in your hotel room. I'd like to come visit with you a few minutes if you don't mind."

"Of course. Come, I'd enjoy a little company," he smiled as he looked at his body. He was naked. On one of the twin beds, he had spread the million dollars in one-hundred dollar bills, and had been rolling around naked over it.

Dan and Kathleen went down and found a waiting taxi. He told the driver to go to the Nile Plaza. Upon arrival, they went straight to Webber's room. It was just that, a single room. Dan knocked, and Webber opened the door.

"This is a surprise. I never expected a couple on their honeymoon to visit me, come in."

They entered, and Webber had arranged two straight backed chairs to face one of the twin beds in the room. Webber said, "Please, take the chairs. I'll sit on the bed. It's a small room."

Dan said, "Thank you," and he and Kathleen sat. The room was all neat and in order. There was nothing out of character with the room.

"What have you come to visit about?"

Dan leaned forward, his elbows resting on his knees, and he fixed Webber with his most piercing stare, "I just came from visiting Mr. Case about the Ramses scarab. I'll tell you what I told Justin. I believe that if the Egyptian Government knew of the Ramses scarab, they would never let it leave Egypt, but would proudly display it in the Cairo Museum. They no longer allow their treasures to be plundered as they once were."

Webber interrupted Dan to respond. "But they know nothing of it. It is just a scarab, and I deal mostly in scarab finds."

"But the Ramses scarab is not 'just a scarab,' it is extremely valuable. It is a great treasure of antiquity."

"But I've already sold it. I don't have it. It's not my problem anymore."

"I beg to differ; you are very much involved. You stole it from Nekhtou, he stole it from a young archaeology student. I believe Nekhtou killed the student for it, and you killed Nekhtou for it. I believe the authorities will arrest you and Justin for attempted theft of an antiquity and murder."

Webber stood suddenly, and shouted, "Get out of here, now! I won't hear any more of your wild accusations. You have no proof of anything. If you go to the police, neither Justin nor I will admit knowing anything you accuse us of. It's just your speculation."

Dan and Kathleen stood and headed toward the door, but Dan posed a thought, "Perhaps you are right, but if told to the police, I believe there would be a major investigation. They *will* learn the truth." With that, Dan and Kathleen left. On their way out, he said, "Now we will see what falls out."

Chapter 14

THE FALLOUT

Thursday morning, June 13, 1985, Cairo, Egypt.

At eight a.m., Cliupatra rose from her bed and padded barefoot into her bathroom. She drew a hot bath, adding perfume. She slipped out of her nightgown and observed herself in the full-length mirror on the bathroom door. She was very pleased at what she saw. At the age of 39, her body was still youthful, slim, and lovely. Her face was also very pretty, her long, dark hair had no gray, not even a thread that she could see. She turned and got into the tub, the water near the top. After she laid down in the warm water, she gave no thought about her late husband, though she had hated him from the day she was forced to marry him in an arranged marriage. Nekhtou was twenty-five years older than she and looked much older than he was. He'd been abusive physically and mentally. She luxuriated in the water as she bathed. She took her own sweet time, then got out and dried, then walked naked back to her room and dressed for the day. When she walked into the kitchen, Jomana had made breakfast for them. Cliupatra sat at their kitchen table. Jomana served their breakfast of eggs cooked in ghee. The women loved the strong Egyptian tea.

"I'm so glad you suggested I go to the police with my problems, Jomana. I feel so much better this morning, as though a burden has been lifted from my heart. Thank you."

"It was all I could think of to do, Cliupatra. I, too, feel relieved."

"Would you go with me?"

"Certainly. We can drop Aksu off at the Bazaar, he can play with his friends there till we are done. The children are all watched closely."

"Good," said Cliupatra.

Jomana went to wake Aksu and feed him breakfast. Then they left, reaching Police Headquarters just after ten. They were taken immediately to speak with the chief detective investigating the murder of Cliupatra's husband. Their female escort was a police officer who introduced them to the detectives. They spoke in Masri.

"Detective Ma'nakhtuf, this is Mrs. Cliupatra Gamal, and her niece, Jomana Gamal. They wish to speak to you about the death of Cliupatra's husband, Nekhtou."

The detective stood. He was a big brawny Egyptian with bushy hair and eyebrows. His hair was still very dark though he was sixty-one years old.

"Good morning, ladies, sit, please. I am very sorry for your terrible loss, Mrs. Gamal."

When they sat, their escort left.

"Now, what may I do for you, Mrs. Gamal?"

Jomana placed her hand over on Cliupatra's hand resting on her leg. It was a gesture of encouragement, so Cliupatra took a deep breath and said, "I have had some very disturbing and frightening things happen to me yesterday, and I think they were all connected to my husband's murder."

The big detective frowned deeply, "What sort of things?"

Cliupatra looked at Jomana who took her hand and squeezed it. "I was first visited by a woman named Mrs. Dan Good. She told me she knew my husband killed that young student from America, and that she knew who murdered Nekhtou and why."

The detective, of course, knew of Dan Good. He'd come to the briefing yesterday, was snubbed and left.

Detective Ma'nakhtuf was puzzled, "It was *Mrs.* Good that said this?"

"Yes," said Cliupatra. "Then later, a Mr. Webber stopped by our shop in the bazaar and indicated he and my husband were in some secret business where my husband made much money, much more than he made from his little jewelry store in the bazaar. He wanted me to make the same arrangement with him as my husband. I believe what they had been doing was illegal. I didn't know what to do but come tell you. I want no part in any of it. She shop is now mine, and I just want to work in it only. Do you understand?"

"I do indeed, Mrs. Gamal. I am very glad you came to us. We will take it from here. You just ignore those people who frightened you. We will protect you. I will assign someone to watch your home and shop."

Cliupatra felt great relief. It had been the right thing to do, thanks to Jomana. They made their farewells and left to go back to the shop and Aksu.

Detective Ma'nakhtuf turned to his partner at the desk next to his, "Were you able to hear everything, Mustafa?"

"Yes. I heard. We must go and have a talk with Mr. Webber very soon, and also Mr. and Mrs. Good."

Justin Case was also very frightened by what Dan Good had said to him. He was so worried he wasn't hungry, didn't even think of breakfast. The ex-lawyer began pacing the floor in his suite, and talking out loud to himself, "The meddling fool. I wish I'd never met Dan Good. It is none of his business. I know he is a private detective, but in Dallas, not in Egypt. He has no right. But what if he does go to the police? They will investigate, and surely they will catch us. I don't want to get mixed up in criminal activity in Egypt. I know what to do, I'm going to go home."

Suddenly he stopped at the telephone table, picked up the receiver and began dialing, "I must warn Webber," he said.

Webber answered on the first ring. Justin spoke before Webber could even say hello, "Will. Has Dan Good talked to you yet?"

"Yes, he and his wife came by my place yesterday, why?"

"Did he threaten you in any way?"

"Yeah, sort of. He said our deal with the Ramses scarab was illegal, and if the Egyptian Government knew they would arrest us both."

"What did you tell him?"

"That all we'd have to do was deny any knowledge. He has no proof of anything. It would be just his word against ours. Don't worry about a thing, Justin."

"But I am worried," responded Justin, "if he went to the police, they would certainly investigate, and I believe you and I might be arrested. I warn you it would be much worse being in an Egyptian jail than an American jail."

"What are you going to do?"

"I'm going home. I suggest you do the same."

Justin hung up. Webber sat down, stunned. Then he began rethinking the situation and became agitated. He stood for a moment, thinking. Wilson Walker Webber was not frightened at all, he was more than angry, he was furious. He, too, paced the floor and spoke to himself aloud, cursing and swearing. "What can I do about Dan Good and his nosiness. How can he be so brash as to meddle in other people's business? He is, however, as Justin said, a very serious threat. How can he be stopped?" Webber stopped pacing. He smiled and sat down. He'd thought of a way, "I'll kill him and his wife."

Chapter 15

THE PROCESS OF MURDER

Friday morning, June 14, 1985, Cairo, Egypt.

When Webber woke, he began thinking again about murdering Dan and Kathleen. How can I kill them? He remembered ways to murder from murder mysteries he'd read, like making the murder appear to be only an accident or suicide. He could not envision himself doing such a thing to Dan and Kathleen. That would also take a lot of time and planning. Strangling was out, Dan was far too big and strong. He was sure he couldn't push them off a high precipice for the same reason. He knew he couldn't shoot them and make it look like murder and suicide. Then he thought he might be able to just shoot them, but not up close. He would have to shoot them from a distance, so he could get away without getting caught. He had his Glock, but a handgun he knew would not be effective at long distance, and he had no rifle. He decided he would have to go find a rifle he could buy, but where? He couldn't go to any gun store. Ah! He knew where to go to find a rifle that could not be traced, Clot Bey Street. It was a dangerous place, but he would be careful.

He went out to his rental car, and drove away, heading for Clot Bay Street to buy a rifle. He had no idea Saphet was following him.

It took him a while, but he finally found a parking spot. He sat for a moment, looking at the people on the streets walking. They were a scruffy looking bunch. This was indeed a place he shouldn't be. Eventually, he gathered his courage, got out of his car, and locked it. He worried that his rental car might be stripped when he returned, or even stolen, but there wasn't anything he could do about that.

With some trepidation, he left the car and began walking. He eyed all the people walking toward him as well as those passing him. You couldn't be too careful in this part of Cairo. There was every kind of store one could imagine along this block, but up ahead, Webber spotted a junk store. It had all kinds of junk for sale, and there was a man out front hawking customers.

He wondered if the store sold guns and decided to ask the man out front.

Webber walked right up to the man, a husky Egyptian with a face like a bandit, he thought. "Pardon me, but do you speak English?"

The man glared at him for almost a minute before he spoke. "Yes, American. What do you want?"

With some relief, Webber decided just to get straight to the point, "I need to buy a rifle. Would you have one for sale?"

The man frowned and cocked his head, "Why you want a rifle?"

Webber became brazen, "I want to kill someone," he answered with a smile as if it were a joke.

The frown deepened, "Who you want to kill, American?"

"An American," he replied, maintaining his smile.

The Egyptian's eyes widened in astonishment. Then he, too, smiled. "Come with me."

Webber followed him into the store. It was crowded. There were piles of many different things everywhere, making it hard to pass through. Customers were plentiful as were salespeople, all jabbering loudly in Masri.

They wriggled their way to the back of the store to a door. The Egyptian opened the door, ushering Webber inside. The room was a large storage facility, and he was led to a big cabinet. The Egyptian opened the double doors and there were stored all kinds of weapons. He took a long rifle off the wall and handed it to Webber.

"This is perfect for you."

The Egyptian didn't bother telling Webber anything about the gun. He deemed Webber an ignorant fool, knowing nothing at all about guns. He was absolutely right, though Webber had a Glock, he knew very little about guns.

Webber took the rifle, looked it over a bit, then asked, "You have bullets for it?"

Without a word, the man picked up a couple of boxes of shells and handed them to him.

"I know nothing about guns, could you show mw how it works, please."

"Of course," he said, taking the gun and shells. Then he spent almost forty-five minutes showing Webber how it worked and letting him do things for himself, until the Egyptian felt he could load and shoot it. Then he said, "I think it would be wise for you to do some target practice till you are sure you can hit what you shoot at. You can go out into the dessert far from people and take some things to shoot at for practice."

Webber blinked. That was the most the man had said to him, but he was grateful, because that was a very good idea.

"I think I will need more bullets."

"Cartridges," thought the Egyptian. He gave him a good supply.

Webber paid the price the Egyptian first mentioned, not realizing the man would bargain with him. Thus, Webber paid far too much, but he went happily on his way back to his car. The Egyptian had put the rifle and ammunition in a large, heavy cloth bag for him.

His car was still where he'd parked it, and he walked around it to see that it was unscathed. He was quite relieved and happy he was successful and had not murdered. He was still unaware Saphet was still following him.

The Cairo police had Webber's hotel staked out, but he chose not to return to his room. Instead, he went around to back alleys, picking up cans, bottles, and other things he thought would make good targets. When he thought he had enough, he headed out to the desert. Saphet had followed and watched him, and when he understood what Webber had in mind, he went back to his little rug shop in the bazaar.

Webber found an area he thought suitable and began his target practice. He soon realized what a terrible shot he was. After a couple of hours, he was hot, sweaty, sandy, and miserable. He decided he would never be able to kill then an any great distance. He must be fairly close to be accurate. Still, he believed his rifle would at least allow him enough distance that he could escape. He was satisfied enough to go back to town.

He stopped at a service station for gas and freshened up as good as he could in the public restroom. He picked up a sandwich from a street vendor for lunch, and, again, instead of returning to his hotel room, Webber decided to go to the NILE Ritz-Carlton Hotel where Dan and Kathleen were staying. He wanted to "case the joint" for a place outside that he thought he could hide, not too far away, and shoot them and get away. This little exercise took him another hour or more.

There was no convenient place he could find, so he decided he would just have to park in the street near the entrance and shoot from a car window, then drive quickly away. It was the best he could do, so he headed back to his room to get a bath and a fresh seersucker suit.

Chapter 16

ARRESTED DEVELOPMENT

It was late afternoon when Webber returned to his hotel. He was hot, tired, and dirty, longing for a nice bath and then dinner at his favorite restaurant, the Maison Thomas pizzeria.

But, as he got out of his car, he was approached by two men in business suits. The big guy with the black bushy hair and eyebrows held up a hand, "Mr. Webber. I am Detective Ma'nakhtuf of the Cairo Police, may we have a word, sir?"

Webber was puzzled, "Police? What's this about? I haven't done anything."

"This is my partner, Detective Mostafa. You must come with us. You are not being arrested; we want to bring you in for questioning."

"No," yelled Webber. "I demand to see the American Ambassador. Take me to the

American Embassy. I've done nothing wrong."

"Sorry, sir, but you are coming with us to Police Headquarters for questioning. If you don't cooperate, we will arrest you on suspicion of murder."

"Murder! No! I haven't murdered anyone, I'm innocent. I am an American citizen. I demand you take me to the American Embassy."

"Do we have to handcuff you?"

Webber wilted. "No."

They put him in the back seat of their car and drove him to Headquarters. At Police Headquarters, Webber was placed in an interrogation room. He was terrified. He'd heard they practiced police brutality in Egypt. He was extremely nervous and fidgety as he sat alone and waited. He jumped like he'd been shot at when the door opened and the two detectives strode in and sat across the table from him.

The detectives stared at him for several moments. Then the big one said, "Mr. Webber. We have reason to believe you murdered Mr. Nekhtou Gamal. We have two who have told us you did. Did you?"

Webber dropped his head so they could not see his eyes, "No, I did not. Who said I killed anyone? I never killed anyone in my life. I'm not a murderer, I'm just a professor of archaeology. I don't know what you are talking about. Have you called the American Embassy for me?"

Ignoring him, Detective Ma'nakhtuf said, "Did Mr. Gamal murder the young American student?"

He shook his head side to side, "Why ask me? I have no knowledge of what Mr. Gamal may or may not have done. Do you have any proof I killed Mr. Gamal? Any eye witnesses?"

"Unfortunately, we do not," said Detective Ma'nakhtuf.

"Then I demand you let me go."

"Not just yet, Mr. Webber. We are keeping you until you confess. I believe you murdered Mr. Gamal." Turning to his partner, Detective Ma'nakhtuf said, "Take him down to the holding cell. I want to call Mr. Good."

Mostafa got up and took Webber downstairs to the holding cell and put him inside.

Webber stood like a statue at the cell door. He looked all around the large cell. There were probably twenty-five or thirty men milling around, but when they noticed Webber, they began walking slowly up to him one by one, giving him the eye. Every face seemed fierce and full of hatred. All were Egyptians of every shape and size. The longer he stood there, the more terrified he became. His heart was pounding like a hammer in his chest, and his head began to hurt. He began to tremble with fear. He couldn't stop himself. Fearing for his life, Webber began shouting for help. No one came. He couldn't understand why, then it dawned on him. None of the guards spoke English. They did not understand what he was yelling about.

An hour later, the envoy from the American came with an American lawyer in tow. Two armed guards went inside to find Webber. They found him slumped in the far corner of the cell, twisted, beaten to a pulp and with a broken neck. He was dead.

The curse continued.

Chapter 17

MORE FALLOUT

Saturday morning, June 15, 1985.

Detective Ma'nakhtuf and his partner, Detective Mostafa were deeply disturbed that Webber was killed while in custody. There was nothing they could do about it now. The attaché from the America was incensed and had raised a big ruckus about it last night, and there would be repercussions from the Americans.

"Oh, well," thought Detective Ma'nakhtuf. It wasn't the first time. They were still very upset about the young American student, but all of that was Lieutenant General Omar's problem.

"Why don't we go see Mr. and Mrs. Dan Good," suggested Detective Mostafa.

"Excellent idea, but we should wait a while. It is Saturday morning, and they are newlyweds."

Dan woke first, and roused Kathleen, "Honey, wake up."

She opened one eye to peek through some blond curls that had fallen across her face. She said, sleepily, "Who are you?"

He grinned and said, "I's me. Is that you?"

She groaned and stretched her lovely arms, "I think so."

"I know it is a bit early, sweetheart, but there is something I want us to do this morning."

She raised up on one elbow, blew a curl away from her face and said, "What?"

"I want to go to Police Headquarters, to see if there has been any fallout from our bone rattling."

She frowned, "On a Saturday morning? You think Police Headquarters is open today, and any detectives working?"

He chuckled, "Of course they're open and cops of every kind are there. Crime doesn't take weekends off."

"I suppose not. Let's take a shower first."

When they had dress to go out, there was a knock on their door, and when he opened it there were two men in business suites.

"Mr. Good?"

"Yes?"

"I am Detective Ma'nakhtuf, and this is my associate, Detective Mostafa. May we visit with you?" He could see Mrs. Good standing behind him. They were both well dressed. He presumed they might be going out for brunch.

"Of course, sirs, come in. We were just going to Police Headquarters. Have a seat anywhere."

The detectives sat side by side on a sofa. Dan and Kathleen sat in wingback chairs facing the sofa; a coffee table between them.

"Would you gentlemen like something to drink? I have coffee and tea," said Kathleen, "and soft drinks," she added.

Both men raise a hand to indicate, stop, Detective Ma'nakhtuf said, "No, thank you, mam, we are quite fine. Why were you going to Police Headquarters if I may ask?"

"First," said Dan, "tell us why you came to see us. If something was important enough for you come here, you should speak first." It was obvious Detective Ma'nakhtuf was the lead detective. Sure enough, he spoke.

"Alright. Yesterday a Mrs. Cliupatra Gamal came to see us." He glanced quickly at his partner. "She told us a rather bizarre story. She said your wife," and he turned his attention to Kathleen and continued. "She said you, Mrs. Good, came to Mr. Gamal's little jewelry store yesterday and told her you believed her husband had killed that young American student, and that you believed you knew who killed her husband and why. Was she correct? Is That about what you said to her?"

Kathleen kept her face bland, nodded, and said, "Yes. I did."

Detective Ma'nakhtuf frowned, "And why did you tell her that? Do you really know her husband killed the young

American, and do you know who killed her husband and why?"

Kathleen looked down, shook her head and said, "No, sir. I have no direct knowledge of anything."

He leaned forward, "Then why did you tell her lies?"

Dan took over, "We have only our suspicions based on a few things we do know, detectives."

"I see," said Detective Ma'nakhtuf. Then, he shook his head, "No. I'm afraid I do not see. Could you be more forthcoming, please."

Dan sat forward, resting his forearms on his thighs, "Yes. I will tell you what we know and what we merely suspect. This is exactly why we were coming to Police Headquarters this morning. First I want to ask you a question. Do you know anything about a scarab of Ramses II?"

The two Egyptians were profoundly taken aback. Their eyes were big as saucers. "What? The scarab of Ramses II? Of course we have heard of it. It is in our school history books. Every Egyptian knows of it. What about it?"

"I'm sorry if I shocked you by that question, but the Ramses scarab is at the center of everything I must tell you. You may be further shocked to learn that the Ramses scarab has been found."

The detectives were more shocked, and Detective Mostafa said, "It was stolen from the tomb of Ramses II about 3,000 years ago, and not known of since. Some have denied the stories of it are even true. Many believe they are just legends. You say it has been found?"

"I have no personal knowledge of it, but hearsay says that the young American archaeology student found it on that dig of the professor and students from Princeton were doing, but he was alone when he found it and sneaked it out to try to sell it to Nekhtou who has been fencing Egyptian artifacts illegally for years. It is my belief Nekhtou killed the student to keep from paying him a finder's fee. I have never seen the Ramses scarab, so I do not know it has been found. I have no proof Nekhtou killed the student."

Detective Ma'nakhtuf asked, "Then why do to think it exists and has been found?"

"Because I met a very wealthy American who told me the scarab has been found and he planned to buy it from his broker. Then I met the broker who said he had it and was going to sell it to the wealthy American. I think the broker killed Nekhtou also to keep from paying him a very large finder's fee."

"And just who are these men, the wealthy American and the broker?"

"The wealthy American is a Mr. Justin Case, and his broker is Professor Wilson Webber."

The detectives were startled again. "Mrs. Gamal mentioned Mr. Webber who frightened her, and we picked him up for questioning last night. We put him in a holding cell overnight to question him again this morning, but he was murdered in the cell last night."

"Webber was murdered?"

"Oh, no," said Kathleen. "That poor man."

"Did you not search Webbers room?"

"Of course we did," said Detective Ma'nakhtuf. "We found no scarab, but we did find a million US dollars in one-hundred dollar bills in a closet."

"He'd already delivered the Ramses scarab to Mr. Case. I think, if you go to Case's suite in this hotel, you will find the scarab."

"Thank you Mr. Good. I believe you are correct in your suspicions. It just makes sense, even without proof. The murders have been solved, I think, and we must confiscate the Ramses scarab before he takes it out of our country." With that the two detectives stood to leave. "You are indeed a brilliant detective, Mr. Good. You live up to your American reputation. I think our Lieutenant General Omar was a fool to snub you, and I apologize."

They made their goodbyes and left, but by the time they went to Case's rooms he was gone. In the lobby they learned he'd checked out and gone to the airport to fly back to the U.S. At Cairo International airport, they learned they were too late. Case's plane was long gone.

After the detectives left, Dan said, "Have you had enough of Egypt, sweetheart?"

Kathleen sighed, "Oh, yes. I'm ready to go home. I feel it will be much more peaceful in our beautiful home. Besides, I miss the Wilsons, they are both so sweet."

"Yes," said Dan. "The Wilsons were with my family before I was born. They have taken very good care of me, especially after my parents were killed. Dotty is glad for you to do most of the cooking, and Brey is happy just doddering around playing at butler and valet."

"I do love to cook and sew."

"You are an unbelievably great cook and seamstress, honey."

"Thank you, kind sir."

"Well, I'm calling for the next flight out, then we can pack."

At 30,000 feet, Justin Case was comfortably ensconced in the first-class section of a big 707, sipping coffee. He was so happy to be on his way home. He did not want his precious scarab far from him, so he had repackaged it and the documents in a smaller, more secure container and stashed in the overhead just over his head. He wasn't about to give up his scarab to anyone, it was his. He'd paid a million dollars for it.

Back in coach, sat Saphet. He had learned Case's name, and that he had checked out of his hotel and gone to the airport to take a flight home. He had learned all this and more from his friends who worked at the NILE Ritz-Carlton Hotel, and his friends at Cairo International Airport. He had even learned Case's home address in Austin, Texas. He was quite pleased with himself. He'd heard that Webber had been murdered in jail, and he was certain they had the million in cash. He was extremely disappointed he had not stolen it from him before he was murdered. All that was left was the Ramses scarab. Saphet, however, was still obsessed to own the scarab. He would never sell it. He planned to take it from Case at his first opportunity. He had closed his little rug shop in the bazaar when he began following Webber. He would open it again when he returned to Cairo with the scarab. He would still have to make a living. At least, he thought, the Ramses scarab would be back in Egypt where it belonged.

The next morning, Dan and Kathleen arrived at the airport early and had time to kill before their flight left. They browsed around for a long time, then, suddenly, they heard Dan's name echoing through the terminal that he had a telephone call. Dan went immediately to the nearest phone.

Kathleen could not even hear Dan's side of the conversation for all the noise in the terminal. She was troubled by the call. Who could it be? Then, Dan hung up.

Kathleen asked, "Who was it, honey?"

"It was Detective Ma'nakhtuf. He asked me to go to Austin and try to convince Justin to return the scarab to the Egyptian government. He wants somebody, Justin, or me, I think, to bring it back to Cairo. He doesn't trust the mail."

"What did you tell him?"

"I said I would try. What else would I say?"

"You done good, fella'. But I want to be in on all of it. I don't want to miss a thing."

Dan smiled at her, "Of course you don't, nosy."

They went hand in hand to find a seat near their gate.

Chapter 18

AND THE CURSE GOES ON, OR DOES IT?

Monday morning, June 17, 1985, Austin, Texas.

Justin Case woke at eight-twenty-eight to go to the bathroom. When he returned, he decided not to go back to bed. He turned on his bedside lamp and went back to the bathroom to take a shower and get dressed for the day. He had not had much sleep, but he was anxious to see his new scarab again.

His longtime housekeeper, Esther, a German immigrant, heard him, but she was already dressed and ready for her day. Esther was just three years younger than her employer and had been working as his housekeeper and cook for seven years. Unknown to him, she had fallen in love with him, though she was far too shy to let him find out how she felt. She believed herself still an attractive woman and hoped Mr. Case did too. He would soon come to the kitchen for breakfast, so she went there and began cooking his favorite, bacon and eggs, coffee, toast, and strawberry jam.

He wandered in as Esther was almost finished putting everything on the breakfast table. As he expected, coffee was made, so he got his favorite mug and filled it, carrying it to the table. He sat, looked over his breakfast all neatly set, looked up at Esther and said, "Thank you, Esther. This looks perfectly wonderful." It made her heart flutter. She smiled back at him, "You are very welcome, Mr. Case." Then she turned to leave. Absently, he began eating and looking at the morning newspaper she had laid next to his plate.

Justin's home was a beautifully restored mansion in the elite section of Austin, known as Hyde Park. The ceilings were ten feet in height throughout his home. On the corner of his block was one of the beautiful Moonlight Towers. They are one-hundred-sixty-five feet tall, and cast light from six carbon arc lamps, illuminating a fifteen-hundred foot radius of light at night so bright that you can read by them. He had arrived late Sunday night. His flight had taken him over sixteen hours due to delays.

After a leisurely breakfast and perusing if the Austin American Statesman, he ambled to a room at the back of his house that was his study. There, he opened his safe and retrieved his package he'd put in it last night when he had returned. He laid the package on his desk and, with his small but very sharp little pocketknife opened the package and removed the scarab and documents. He carefully laid the documents in his safe. They were all in hieroglyphics that he could not read. He threw the wrappings in a trash can and set the Ramses scarab on the desk in front of him.

On a table next to his desk was his collection of scarabs in display. He would rearrange the display to make room for its center piece, the huge Ramses scarab, but first, he wanted to just sit and look at it.

Once again, he was amazed at the enormous size of it, far, far larger than any other scarabs in his collection, far larger than any he'd ever seen. Its great beauty dazzled him. He admired it for several minutes, then he thought, "It is MINE! Mine alone!"

Then he suddenly realized, *"I can't display it. No one else must see it."* Disappointment sat on him like a granite boulder. He sighed deeply. *"I never thought about the fact I could never show it. Dan Good was right, I did obtain it illegally, and that is why I must keep it a secret. I can't believe I spent a million dollars for something I can't brag about. I thought I would have*

my picture with the scarab on the front page
of all major newspapers. I'm a fool. Why
have it if I can't show it to everybody? It is
absolutely useless. Dan was also right
again when he said it should belong to the
Egyptians. It should be displayed in their
great museum and marveled at by millions.

Just then, the doorbell rang. He frowned. *"Esther will answer it,"* he thought. Still, he sat admiring the beautiful artifact. In a very few moments, he heard a knock on his study door. That troubled him. Esther would never interrupt him when he was in his study unless it was something of great importance. "What, Esther?"

"I'm sorry to bother you Mr. Case, but you have a visitor."

"I don't want any visitors today, Esther, tell them to go away, please."

"He won't go away, Mr. Case," she said, but her voice sounded strained.

"Who is it? Who won't go away?"

"I don't know the man, Mr. Case, he won't tell me his name."

Justin thought for a moment, then thought he would just tell her to come in, but his door was locked. He would have to get up. This made him angry.

With a bit of exasperation, he said, "I'm not seeing anyone today, Esther, do you understand? Tell him to go away."

"I'm sorry, Mr. Case, but if you don't open this door now, he is going to hurt me bad."

He was shocked, "Hurt you? I can't believe this."

Justin stood up, "Just a moment, I'm coming."

Just as he unlocked the door, it came crashing open and a big husky Egyptian man hustled Esther in in front of him. He held her tightly to himself and held a knife to her throat. They crashed into Justin who stumbled back against his desk.

The Egyptian shouted, "Don't move or I will slit her throat."

Justin righted himself but pressed himself against his desk. "What is this? What do you want?"

He looked at Justin's desk, "I see what I want. The Ramses scarab."

Without thinking, Justin shouted, "No! You can't have it, it's mine!"

"If you don't give it to me now, I will cut her throat and then yours," he threatened.

"Alright, alright," said Justin. "I'll give it to you, just don't hurt her." He sidled around his desk, picked up the heavy object and tossed it to him, causing the big man to let Esther loose so he could catch the big scarab. Esther wrenched herself free, turned and ran out the door. Saphet dropped the scarab on the carpet. Then in a rage, lunged at Justin with his long-bladed knife to stab him in his heart.

Suddenly, there was a loud POP! Saphet's head exploded. Dan Good stood in the doorway, holding a smoking gun. No silencer. Saphet fell like an empty suit to the floor. He did not move.

Esther rushed by him to throw her arms around Justin, "Oh, my love, I thought you were killed. Thank God!" Justin was as surprised as Esther was when she got control of herself. "I'm so sorry, sir," she hung her head in shame. "I don't know what came over me."

"I... I... do..." stammered Justin. "And I am glad, Esther. I have come to love you very much." They embraced as Kathleen entered the study with Dan.

"What's going on? What did I miss?"

"You missed the most important part of this story, sweetheart, the love scene at the end," said Dan.

They all laughed, then sobered quickly. There was a dead body on the floor, and blood was soaking a large area of expensive carpet. When Justin began to settle down, he said, "Mr. Good... Dan. How is it you showed up when you did? It seems a miracle."

"We came back on the very next flight. Before we left, Detective Ma'nakhtuf called me to ask if I would come down to Austin and try to persuade you to return the Ramses scarab to Egypt. If you will, I am to take it back if you can't or don't want to go back. We thought of waiting till tomorrow but decided this morning to just come on down. We drove and got here just in time to see Esther running out the front door. She looked scared to death, so I rushed inside with her close behind me."

He still stood with his arm around Esther's shoulder. "I am... *we* are so glad you did." He looked at her fondly. "It is a shame it took something like this to break the ice between Esther and me, but I am very happy."

Esther looked up at Justin. "And so am I."

Dan bent and picked up the scarab which was still on the floor. "Well, Justin, what about it? The Ramses scarab?"

"I have decided to return it. I will to go in the next day or so."

Kathleen chimed in, "Oh, Justin, I'm so proud of you."

Justin squeezed Esther a little tighter, "But now I have someone to go to Egypt with me."

Esther took in a sudden deep gasp of air. "Oh, Justin!"

"I'm sorry to break you two apart, but we need to call the police. There has been a murder, and your carpet is ruined."

"Don't worry about the carpet, Dan, I'll call the police, I'm well acquainted with them, being a criminal defense attorney."

"And I have a very good attorney if I need one," said Dan, and they all laughed.

The police came and their investigation took only a little over an hour. Justin knew the detectives on a first name basis and deftly handled the situation. Dan and Kathleen were impressed.

After they left, Justin turned to Esther and said, "Esther, my dear, we've known each other for years. I see no reason I shouldn't ask you to marry me here and now, in front of God and everybody." He glace at Dan and Kathleen.

"Of course I will marry you. I have loved you a very long time."

Justin smiled and said, "I doubt many have proposed marriage to a woman at a murder scene." That really broke everyone up.

Dan and Kathleen took them out to a nice restaurant some distance away, across the bridge over the Colorado River to the Night Hawk on South Congress Avenue. It was Justin's favorite place.

After much discussion, Justin and Esther decided to leave for Cairo in a couple of days. Neither wanted a big wedding, in fact, they didn't want to wait, and decided to let a Justice of the Peace Justin knew perform their wedding, and to go to Cairo for their honeymoon as Dan and Kathleen had done.

"By the way, Justin," said Kathleen. "We bought a couple of nice scarabs while we were there, but we don't really want to become collectors. We paid nine-hundred apiece for them. We thought we would give them to you for your collection if you want them."

"Let me see them."

She took them out of her purse and handed them to him. Justin took them and looked them over very carefully, then handed them back to Kathleen, "These are fakes. They are worth just a very few dollars, I'm sorry to tell you.."

Dan and Kathleen were stunned. Dan said, "That Nekhtou was as crooked as a corkscrew."

Shortly after lunch, Dan and Kathleen went back to Dallas. As they rode along in Dan's big Cadillac he said, "Well, I guess that is the end of our adventure of the Ramses scarab."

They rode in silence a few miles, then Kathleen cocked her head at Dan and said, "I wouldn't count on that."

EPILOGUE

The newlyweds, Justin, and Esther sat in seats near their gate. It would be another fifteen or twenty minutes before they would board their flight to Cairo. Justin had packaged the Ramses scarab documents in a box with bubble wrap protection. He had checked it with their suitcases. Esther had made the box look like a very nice present to present to the Egyptian government. Justin kept it close to him at all times. Esther carried her makeup case, planning to put it in the overhead when Justin put his package there. They sat silently holding hands as they watched the planes land and take off from DF/W.

After about five minutes they noticed a commotion of some sort in the terminal, but what caught their attention was the activity on the runway just in front of them. A firetruck appeared with lights and sirens. And men began spraying foam over the area. Two paramedic trucks sped into position.

Justin and Esther got up and walked to the big window to search the sky, thinking there must be a plane in trouble. They saw it. A small private plane coming in low for a landing, but it was a three-wheeler, and the front landing gear had not folded out. It was stuck. The plane was about to make a crash-landing right in front of them. People could get killed, and the plane might explode in flames. This was a terrible thing to watch, but Justin and Esther could not budge. A crowd of people had gathered all around them to watch.

The plane landed with only the two wheals touching down. It slowed, and soon the nose without a wheel nosed down hitting the ground, skidding through the foam. Fortunately, the plane didn't catch fire. It finally came to a stop. Quickly, the passengers were helped out and taken away from the plane. There had been a young family in the plane, a father and mother and three small children, all alive and safe. The lobby thundered with cheers, clapping, shouting, and laughter.

Justin and Esther were greatly relieved and turned to go back to their seats. People moved out of their way, going back to their previous places. But Justin and Esther were shocked to see his package was gone. Someone had stolen it while they were watching the excitement.

"Oh, Justin. What are we to do?"

He looked around, hoping to see someone with it, but there was no one.

"Well," he said, "I see no point in reporting it stolen, hon. All they got was the scarab. I doubt very much if the police could ever catch who took it. They are probably long gone by now. I guess I can't return what I don't have, but we can still enjoy a wonderful honeymoon in Cairo."

The boarding call resounded over the speaker system. As they casually joined those boarding, Justin thought to himself: *"That curse may actually be valid. The young man who found it was murdered as was Webber and his broker. I wonder if the thief that stole it will die."* Then another thought came to him unbidden: *"I wonder how soon I will die."*

ABOUT THE AUTHOR

Richard Norman was born in 1929 in the Rio Grande Valley of Texas. He married in 1949, and they had six children. His wife died in 2010, and oldest son died in 2019 at the age of 68. He was a banker, a commercial artist and a minister. He sang in symphony choruses for 35 years, and two years in the Dallas Opera. He retired in 2008 at the age of 78. At age 83 he began writing, and has written 40 books, most of which have been published. He is currently working on his fourth novel, The Primitive Predator. He sings every day on Sing Snap, a karaoke website. He lives with his youngest son, a twin, Joe, in Coppell, Texas.

Printed in Great Britain
by Amazon